An Inchworm Takes Wing

An Inchworm Takes Wing

Published by Thomas-Jacob Publishing, LLC

TJPub@thomas-jacobpublishing.com

Library of Congress Control Number: 2020949627

1. Contemporary fiction 2. Literary fiction

ISBN-13: 978-1-950750-35-1

ISBN-10: 1-950750-35-3

Thomas-Jacob Publishing, LLC, Deltona, Florida

First hardcover printing Thomas-Jacob Publishing, LLC November 2020

Printed in the United States of America

An Inchworm Takes Wing

by Robert Hays

This book is dedicated to all those
whose most fierce demons reside within their own
minds.

"Above the world is stretched the sky,
no higher than the heart is high."
                          --Edna St. Vincent Millay

1 / *I dream*

I JUST HAD A CLEAR vision of paradise. It was not the heaven you learned about in Sunday School, but nonetheless a peaceful world without war and bloodshed and dead children and temptation and wanton betrayal, and there was no hate and no violence and no deceit and no hurtful repercussions. Nita and Bucky and Marilyn and my children and grandchildren and innocents from the war were there, and I looked them all in the eyes without shame and they looked back and smiled and it was as if those things never happened. But they did. And although I was rescued for a time from all the pain and guilt that permeate my conscious hours, this was only a dream.

I suppose I was sleeping; dreams are said to be the creation of a brain at rest. My dream of paradise mercifully interrupted a more familiar one about war and people dying all around me, a nightmare in which I see and feel and hear and smell the carnage just as I did when it was real. This is my usual dream. It is the one I fear, the one that often causes me to dread the coming of sleep even when I need it and want to and should embrace it.

In the war I learned to treasure sleep like life itself because sleep, when you could get it, was the only temporary respite from the ugliness of the real world stage on which I was an unwitting player. The play may be over now, but my role seems never to go away. It is as if I wait in the wings for my call and there no longer is an escape. I yearn for that peaceful sleep but find it most elusive.

Even though they offer vividly contrasting views of reality, asleep and awake are separated only by the finest of lines in my current state of awareness. I can distinguish one from the other only because at times I hear sound around me or see light or dark above me and moving shapes I think are people. All these, through my wakened senses, are fragmented and uncertain, while perceptions in the dreams that come during sleep are vibrant and unambiguous as if my mind is determined to make me accept a world where what has come and gone or a new universe where things are as I would like them to be is the real here and now.

I hear music. Relentless guitars. Lynyrd Skynyrd, I think. "Free Bird," maybe. Or the Allman Brothers Band, "Ramblin' Man." But sometimes I get confused between the Allman Brothers and the Dooby Brothers. And the music may be only in my head. They wouldn't be playing loud rock music in a hospital, and while my normal senses are muted and my brain may be scrambled and confused I know that's where I am.

I think I have been here, in this hospital, for a day or more, though I have no clear sense of time—days and nights, the real time that controls your life, time you read on the face of a clock or a calendar on the wall. Time over the long span is another matter.

Days and weeks and months and years from the past are as alive in my memory as if they were yesterday. There is so very much I want to forget, but a lifetime of ups and downs plays out endlessly in my head, like a movie that just keeps rewinding and running again and again. No matter how hard I try, I cannot stop it and make it go away.

Say what you will about hospitals, they have morphine. Or maybe something new I haven't heard about. I'm no authority on drugs—legal drugs, in any case—but whatever it is they are dripping into my veins, I feel no physical pain.

My body is battered and I sense I am being kept alive only by modern medicine and medical technology and those skilled in their use. God bless them—though I should feel hypocritical even to express this thought. God and I don't communicate anymore. I'm sure He's had enough of me and I have my doubts about Him.

My grandmother would say God was with me in the wreck, otherwise I would not be here now. I'm inclined to think it was the care of first responders or maybe nothing more than luck or fate or whatever you want to call it, rather than the hand of God. It doesn't matter. I survived. Marilyn still has a husband, Annie and Craig a father, the littlest among us a grandfather, and Bucky a best friend.

I remember just before the accident and right up until I knew it was happening, but nothing after that. They say traffic on Interstate 57 always is heavy. It certainly was then. There was a short construction zone in the north-bound lanes and a few miles farther on a second one that seemed endless and we got all bunched up, one vehicle too close to another, and then everything had to be squeezed into single file. All at once there was a speeding eighteen-wheeler in the passing lane and no place to merge and a terrible collision right in front of me. I tried to stop but was rammed hard from behind and then there was a series of grinding chain-reaction crashes, like a fast train running into the side of a mountain and one car slamming into another from front to end.

What had been moving vehicles were left nothing more than a mass of steel and glass and plastic and rubber and leaking fuel tanks ready to burst into flame. My little Subaru was demolished.

I took a merciful blow to my head in the initial impact and everything went black. I didn't feel anything after that. I know I was trapped and I don't know who got me out.

I hope I'm wrong, but I think some of those injured were children. A few miles back I passed a minivan and there were kids in it who waved and I think it was close behind when we got slowed by the construction. Innocent children, with their whole lives yet to live, should not be hurt like I was. If God was going to be with someone, surely He would have been with the children.

This time, I did nothing wrong. The familiar cliché about merely being in the wrong place at the wrong time honestly applies. I wish this was not exceptional, but there have been too many turning points in my life when I had choices and made bad ones. The face in my mirror is that of a man who cannot declare himself a good person. Not an evil man, not one who ever intended to do wrong, but a man who has hurt other human beings when he didn't have to and cannot claim credit even for trying to do the right thing.

I could not have stopped the killing of innocents in the war. But if I had taken a stand, if I had stood up against what I knew was wrong, there might have been others who would have joined my protest and innocent lives might have been spared. I was a coward and did nothing. The blood cannot be washed from my hands. No matter how horrid the nightmares, they are mere reminders of the truth and this truth never shall set me free.

It has been almost five years since I last saw Nita. I still saw Bucky several times a week before we moved and a chance to spend a few days visiting with him was my only reason for this ill-fated trip to Chicago. Bucky is the best friend I've ever had and the six months since we last had any time together seems like years.

Why did I ever think it was a good idea to move? Did I truly expect to crest a brighter horizon, or was I only running away? No matter. The deed is done and now I am terrified at the realization I might never see Bucky again.

I understand why Bucky is the way he is, and I think he understands me. We were not together in combat, never side by side in some swamp or jungle or on a battle-scarred hillside, and he was not present that awful day in that remote village nor a couple of days later when I got hit, but we were in the same war at the same time and came out of it all with pretty much the same wounds to body and spirit. Our war never really has ended. Bucky and I still fight it every day, and I miss having him beside me in our battle now. We've leaned hard on one another through the roughest stretches and it goes without saying that each of us stands ready when the other needs support.

We are not equal in this battle, though. I admire and respect Bucky for the way he fights his demons and I wish I were half as strong. Every man has his breaking point. I can't say I know mine, but I am sure I've come close more than once. I've been to the white room. If I leave this hospital alive I know my ultimate surrender will come before Bucky's, even though I still have Marilyn and he no longer has Nita to cheer him on. Nita was good support in the beginning, but actually added a lot to Bucky's anguish in the end, and to mine, too, because I was part of the mix and Bucky is the last person in the world I ever would deliberately hurt.

Bucky always is straight with me. I cannot make the same claim. One night, when we'd had too many vodka martinis and he went on a crying jag and said he hated himself because he didn't have the guts just to go walk in front of a train and end it all, I almost confessed.

They say conscience is one thing that elevates humans a bit over other animals. I don't think this is entirely true, because I remember how Nita's cat used to try to make up after he'd bitten or scratched her in one of his little temper tantrums, but to the extent it is true I can't help but envy the other animals. My conscience never will be clear.

I don't have many friends left. I'm not comfortable at social events and once I stopped teaching I never felt as if I had much in common with any of the people Marilyn wanted us to hang out with. She probably got tired of trying to think up new excuses and simply quit making commitments. I doubt she would have agreed to leave Chicago and move to the other end of Illinois, nearly four hundred miles distant, had I not become such a social drag. But she thought the forests might help me find peace and she did it for me. Marilyn never has put herself first.

I believe Marilyn loves Bucky almost as much as I do, and I know she considers him among her dearest friends. She pushed me to plan this trip, bought us tickets to a couple of Cubs baseball games, and assured us that she wanted this time for the two of us and she would rather not come. She and I could come back to Chicago any time, she said, but these days were to be ours—Bucky's and mine, alone.

I think Marilyn is here. She will stay by my side just as she always has, no matter what. I love this woman so very much. She deserves someone better than me. I wish I could tell her this, and let her know how much I love her. I want to tell her that no matter how many times I've failed her, it never was her fault. I want to tell her I'm sorry. And one day, maybe, I can tell Bucky, too.

And I need to tell Marilyn everything. I've avoided too long the worst of what I've done, the grim story I'm so ashamed of, afraid that even she could not find it within herself to forgive such a transgression. I've kept from her the sheer horror of that one ghastly day when inhumanity reigned and the unending guilt I've lived with ever since. Not sharing this unbearable secret with the woman who has been the center of my universe has left a barrier between us that I know she feels but cannot understand. I want with all my heart to live to speak to her again and tell her what I should have confessed years ago but didn't, and I can only hope that replacing this darkness with light may finally bring me peace.

2 / Jan and Doctor Morrison

THE PATIENT IN ROOM 12 of the Intensive Care Unit on the sixth floor of Memorial Hospital's Wing C might have been a stone figure in the middle of the cramped enclosure, white and immobile, and bent at the waist as if molded in silhouette to fit the contoured hospital bed. His head and torso were swathed in bandages and his arms and legs were awkwardly positioned in hard casts and layers of heavy gauze wrapping. The ethereal setting was completed by an intricate maze of medical para- phernalia on all sides and overhead and variations of back lighting controlled by a panel of switches on the wall behind the bed.

The nurse moved swiftly about the room, taking and recording vital signs that marked the presence of life. As she typed the last bits of a new day's first mi- nutiae into a computer mounted on a rolling stand at the side of the patient's bed, she was conscious of the very real possibility it might be the final paragraphs of his life story and this awareness made her sad. She found nurs- ing richly rewarding but often stressful.

The compassion she felt for the man lying before her, motionless and without a single overt sign of life, was simple. She never had heard his voice, she never had seen a smile on his face, she never had observed even a modest glimmer of emotion in his eyes. He was flesh and blood and bone, but if some trace of human spirit remained it no longer presented a single visible outward manifestation. But he was her patient. She had taken an oath to devote herself to the welfare of those committed to her care.

She was a slender woman and young, not tall, with black hair and gray eyes and skin like opaque ivory, and though she didn't think of herself as pretty she was aware that the other nurses did and took secret satisfaction in the special attention she got from some of the young male interns. From her earliest memories, she had wanted to care for others. Medical school had been her dream. Growing up in rural Iowa, the youngest of four children, she had tended to take this for granted. She would be a doctor.

But by the time she finished high school, she had a better understanding of the stringent academic preparation necessary for medical school admission and a more realistic recognition of the cost. There was not a lot of science in the curriculum of her small-town schools, and the gap between her family's modest income and medical school tuition looked as wide as the Pacific Ocean. She settled for a community college nursing degree and never looked back. The day she put her training to work in the office of a local family physician was the proudest day of her life.

Fifteen years of nursing, including two years now in the ICU, had not conditioned her to accept easily that sometimes the death of a patient is inevitable. And she had not learned to deal with death without emotion. She wanted nursing to be about life and making people well to enjoy it.

The nurse finished such additions to the record as there were and was about to leave the room when Doctor Arne Morrison stormed in, brushed past her without speaking, and went straight to the bedside computer she had just left. He pushed his glasses back on his forehead and punched awkwardly at the keyboard, then threw up his hands in a gesture of frustration.

"How the hell do I get this screen to come up?" he demanded.

The nurse nudged him aside. She pulled up the patient's information on the computer screen with a few strokes on the keyboard and stepped back.

"It used to be simple," the doctor said. "An actual chart with all the written information I needed at the foot of the bed. When did we get to be totally at the mercy of all this damned high technology, anyway?"

"It has been like this almost as long as I've been in nursing," she told him. "We have a lot more information right here this way, and it's easier to get the background stuff. But you know all this. You just want me think you are a grumpy old man."

"You're just a kid, Janet. Be patient with me. I am an old man, and any nurse in this hospital will tell you I can be very grumpy."

"It's Janice."

"Sorry. I know that. I always want to call you Janet for some reason."

"Call me Jan. Makes it easier. Tough night?"

"Getting to be almost routine. In surgery till whenever—after midnight. Two kids on a motorcycle hit by a car. Damn, I wish they'd get those things off the road. Motorcycles, I mean, not cars."

"I do, too. I'll never let my boys on one."

"Yeah, well good luck on that. The time will always come when you lose control of what your offspring can and can't do. How's our patient this morning?"

"Nothing much different. His blood oxygen is still low, and so far as we can tell he's not been awake yet."

The doctor, a tall, heavy man with stooped shoulders and unruly white hair and intense dark eyes, moved back to the computer and quickly scanned the record page she'd left open on the screen. "This poor guy doesn't have a lot going for him, but we've got to get a read on this low oxygen. Crush injuries are hard to deal with. His heart was bruised but seems to be working properly. There may be pressure on his vagus nerve. Was his wife here?"

Jan nodded. "She was here all night, apparently. I just now persuaded her to go to her motel and get some rest. I tried to pretend he's not as bad as he is, but I think she knows he probably won't make it."

"She knows. I told her that right off."

"I'm sorry. I didn't know. I would not want her to think—"

"The right hand doesn't know what the left hand is doing? That's SOP around here." The doctor drew in a long, deep breath and let it out slowly. "Sometimes I hate this job, Janet. People think we just go about our business saving lives all day, but they forget about the ones we can't save. I hate having to face that wife and tell her there's no hope. Don't get too close to her. That only makes it all the more painful in the end, and you don't need that."

The nurse sipped from a mug of cold coffee she had carried with her into the room. "But how can I not sympathize with her? I try to think how I'd feel if it was Phil lying there. I don't know if I could handle it. Is he set for more surgery?"

"God, I don't know if he can take it. We've got more to do, but I suppose it's mostly palliative. The human body can only take so much punishment and his has had about all it can stand. I don't think I've ever seen anybody as smashed up as he is and still alive before, and I've been at this a long time. But you never know. This guy's pretty tough or he wouldn't be here now. We'll do all we can and hope for the best."

"I'll try to take your advice about his wife. It's just hard—"

"Look, you're a good nurse because you care. The day you stop caring is the day you're no longer a good nurse. Don't let my cynicism mess you up."

"Thank you." She smiled the sweet smile he had always considered ample reward for his advice. "Where are your groupies this morning?"

Doctor Morrison made a face, pretending to be put off by her question. "The medical students? They finished with me and got moved on to another department. I'll have a new crop in a few days, but for now it won't be so crowded in here."

"I thought they seemed like a pretty good bunch."

"They are very promising. A couple of them dedicated to a lifetime of healing the sick, even."

The nurse finished washing her hands at a sink in the corner of the room, dried them with paper towels, and turned back to the doctor. "Sometimes I can't tell whether you're serious or only joking, Doctor Morrison. Aren't all medical students dedicated? Why else would they want to be doctors?"

"Money. Nurses have to be dedicated because they don't make enough money for that to be the attraction, but a lot of medical students still go into the field because they think they will be rich."

"Well, to quote my favorite rich doctor, 'If you say so'."

She put a hand on the patient's shoulder. There was a spot on the upper right thigh where blood had soaked through the heavy gauze that covered the site of a stapled incision.

"Open reduction?" She indicated the stain.

"Right leg and left arm. We probably need to get some fresh packs on there. Is there any other family? Besides his wife, I mean."

"There is a son and daughter and grandchildren, but none of them have been here. I think she expects them to come, though."

11

"I hope they don't wait too long."

"I think they're pretty well scattered. I saw on the computer that we finally caught up on some records on this patient, as I'm sure you know."

The doctor nodded. "We probably don't have it all," he said. "But we got enough to know he was all shot up in Vietnam. You'd think one time around was enough, but now he has to go through this."

"Any possibility of Agent Orange?"

"Not that we can tell, and his wife doesn't think so. But, yes, chemical exposure is still showing up in some of these poor fellows who didn't even realize it could still happen after all this time."

"Poor fellow, is right." Jan lingered over the patient. "I guess he's in God's hands now," she said softly.

"If you say so. I have yet to see God on the surgery ward. I don't mean to be sacrilegious, but I think you and I will have more to do with his survival than God does. No offense if you are a true believer."

"I believe in God."

"Well, God or not, we have to go about our job like we are the only hope the patient has. You on the front end of a shift or about done?"

"Just started."

"Keep the faith, darlin'. We do great medicine here, as I'm sure you've been told. Probably even printed on your paycheck."

"I see it all over. They say it is the Memorial Hospital motto and we are all expected to live up to it. I've always wondered who thought that up."

The doctor smiled, then laughed.

"That all came before my time, hard as it may be for you to believe," he said. "My guess is they spent a million dollars or so on a marketing study by some Chicago consulting firm and the motto is what they got. Patients and their insurance companies probably still paying for that little gem."

Doctor Morrison took another look at the computer screen and shook his head. He turned and walked away slowly, looking down, as if studying the multi-colored pattern on the tiled floor. Once outside the room he walked faster and went straight to the elevators and left the floor. Jan stepped back to the keyboard and began typing. When she'd finished adding new material, she scrolled back over what was already there. She shook her head sadly as she read.

"I don't know how this one has made it this far," she said, speaking only to herself.

3 / *I'm not important*

I WONDER IF ANGELS really sing. I think I hear a drumbeat, but I'm pretty sure it's not the rhythm of a heavenly choir. It's more like the sound of boots, boots, boots, tromping into battle, and I'm afraid I may be caught in Rudyard Kipling's legion of the lost. I am still earth-bound, but how can I be sure I'm not among the damned, a tiny dot afloat in a vast universe and about to be enfolded into the nether clouds of another world?

I should be glad I have no pain, but not being able to feel my own body brings no satisfaction. Pain serves a purpose. It tells us our bodies are alive and our senses are functioning, and without pain there are no signals to alert us when something goes wrong. How would I know if I am broken beyond any hope of repair? I am no longer me, no longer a whole being.

What if I'm already dead and simply can't tell the difference?

But my mind is alive and as long as there is life there is hope. As long as there is life there is the prospect of rebirth. As long as there is life there is promise. Not the promise of a perfect body, but what does this matter? My body has been shattered before, in an earlier time, parts of me decimated by the slings and arrows of war. I survived then, even though I had no right to claim redemption, and there surely is some prospect of survival now.

I never have expected life to be certain. And I've never believed that, in the grand scheme of things, I was particularly important. When I was very young my father told me if I thought I counted for much to go stick my thumb in a glass of water and see how big a hole was left when I pulled it out. That's the only thing I remember him ever telling me, although of course he was not around very long. I heard a lot of guys in the war talking about things they learned from their fathers, but they never heard this from me.

No matter. I'm still here, and I think I know where I am. I know about where I was when the accident happened, and if I've calculated correctly I probably ended up in a hospital in Urbana, Illinois. I think Urbana would have been the closest place with major trauma center medical facilities and if this is where I am they most likely brought me here by air ambulance straight from the crash scene on Interstate 57.

I'm only speculating and I may be wrong, but if this happened it was an encore experience because I had the honor of a medevac rescue in the war. I was conscious during that one and I still remember it like it was only yesterday. It's both one of my worst memories from the war and one of my best.

You'll understand that being hit and nearly dying is among the bad memories. The good memory is that my life was saved by heroic people. My left arm was nearly shot off and I would have bled to death in minutes had it not been for a couple of medics who got to me fast and stopped the bleeding. It was as if, at that moment in time, my life was the most valuable one they had to worry about. I wouldn't have made it had they not got me to a field hospital as soon as they did.

A "dustoff" call, the radio code for medevac, probably already had gone out, not just for me, but I knew my time was running out and that big, black Huey helicopter was a beautiful sight. The pilots slid it in under heavy fire and the image of that giant bird settling down right where we were is as vivid in my mind's eye as if it were happening now. I can hear the monotonous chop, chop whirling of the rotors and feel the rush of wind as it descends.

That medevac crew had to have been easy targets for Vietcong rifles, but they ran out into the open with complete disregard for their own safety to get me loaded and in the air. God, those guys were fantastic! Not only did they save my life, but there have been a lot of times over the years when I found myself running low on hope of ever putting the war behind me and then remembered how they risked their own lives to save mine and felt an obligation not to give up. I owe them at least that.

I suppose it's not uncommon in war, but I never had a chance even to know who rescued me. I wish I knew their names and where they are now and how they have fared in life.

Yes, I know it doesn't seem realistic that I recall all this from the war in such detail and know nothing about the rescue that just brought me here. Unlike the first one, I was out cold this time around. Like before, though, I know I was saved by people I never will come into contact with again, and I can add the cast of my new venture into the realm of near-death experience to my roster of anonymous heroes.

Just like the first time, I never will know who they are and never hear their stories. I'm sorry for that. I wish them all the best and hope they live long and happy lives and, somewhere along the way, get the recognition they deserve for doing what they do. I wish I could meet them all and shake their hands and tell them I'm grateful.

If I'm right about where I am, I've been here before— not the hospital, but the city. Urbana is home to the University of Illinois, more than a hundred miles south of our old home in Chicago and more than double that distance north of our new one down in the Shawnee. Straight up and down Interstate 57, either way. Marilyn and Bucky and Nita and I came down from Chicago a couple of times to Bob Dylan concerts here, and Marilyn and I were here for Neil Diamond and for the first of the Farm Aid concerts organized by Willie Nelson. I remember this one well because nearly every American rock group and solo artist I'd ever heard of performed, and the music went on almost all day and night in a football stadium packed with thousands of rowdy fans.

I don't remember why Bucky and Nita didn't come, but they watched it on television over the Nashville Network and Bucky said they got a glimpse of Marilyn and me in the crowd close in front of the stage. He said Marilyn looked like she belonged on camera and I looked like a confused soul lost in a mass of humanity. Probably the way I felt, too. But the concert was great.

I know this is ancient history, but for Bucky and me Farm Aid was kind of like a substitute for Woodstock. When the real Woodstock took place, we were too busy trying to get our lives moving again after shedding our blood in the war. And we didn't watch the moon landing live on television, either. We saw the video later, and we resented all the money and time and effort to put a man on the moon when they couldn't get us out of Vietnam. Or maybe I should say *wouldn't* get us out.

Marilyn asked me once if I resented missing music concerts and the like that other guys my age were going to when I was in the war. I didn't. I'd never been to a concert and never expected to go to one. When I was growing up, I only knew music on records and on the radio and we got that in Vietnam. Led Zeppelin was a new band, and the first time we heard them Bucky said they were better than the Rolling Stones. I suppose that was a standard we thought couldn't be beat, even if we hadn't seen Mick Jagger's strut. We didn't know Jimi Hendrix then and it was years before Stevie Ray Vaughn.

I didn't agree with him. My contention was that the Stones still were the best, though it was obvious Led Zeppelin would be competitive. We spent hours listening to both.

Yes, this all sounds trite now, but when you spend your days lying around an Army hospital just hoping for better times ahead, any break from the monotony can become a memorable event. We made heroes of those who created our kind of music because they helped us through our darkest hours when we felt like most people didn't care. We used music as a crutch, and to some extent I think we still do. I can get lost in music and everything else goes away.

Things are fading out a bit. I know they think I'm asleep. Since I can't move or communicate with them in any way they probably couldn't tell the difference. I hope I can talk with the doctors when I get through this and let them know my mind still was functioning a lot of the time even if they couldn't tell. Maybe they will learn something that could help somebody else in this condition, or maybe—since I hold out no hope we'll ever not have them—my experience could benefit guys like me who have to go to war and get all shot up.

If I sound like I spend almost every conscious minute thinking about the war, I apologize. It's probably because I'm hurt again that I'm thinking so much about it now. But I won't deny that the war had a profound effect on me. You can't see and do the things you see and do in war and not be changed by it.

I can't recall his exact words right now, but I am trying to remember something John Dryden wrote about pleasure after pain. There is no question the war left me with both physical and mental pain that never will go away, but no amount of pain could excuse the pursuit of pleasure I knew was wrong. I can't blame everything on the war. I knew what I was doing and I knew it was not right.

My grandmother used to say that something good usually comes out of even the worst thing that happens to you, and maybe it's a stretch but in the end the war led me indirectly to a more positive world. I was able to go to college and become a teacher. I'm grateful for this, although at the time I couldn't help but resent that it was a trade-off for making me go to war to begin with. I felt like I was paying my way with blood money.

Uncle Dick used to say if you took all the blood money out of circulation the system would break down. "Just make sure your own hands aren't bloody, boy, and don't worry about everybody else," he told me. "Always give an honest day's work for an honest day's pay and you'll turn out all right."

I wish I could say my hands are not bloody, but I can't. But having been given a chance, I've tried my best always to give an honest day's work. Uncle Dick would be proud of me for that.

I went to Indiana State University in Terre Haute, and over time managed to get settled enough to concentrate on my studies and graduate. Indiana State may not be Harvard, but it has high standards and I'm no genius. I probably wouldn't have made it except for two things. First, Bucky was there, too. And second, and most important, I met Marilyn there and she became a rock of support.

Indiana State gave me a good education. I'm proud that I got a degree and became a teacher. I've dedicated my life to working with girls and boys and I truly believe there were times I made a difference. Teaching let me share a love of poetry and literature I gained from my grandmother when I was a child. I thought of her often as I stood in my classroom in Chicago and hoped my students might take away even a small part of the pleasure in these which was my gift from her. I could almost hear her soft, gentle voice reading her favorite poems by Alfred, Lord Tennyson, and wished she could know how her influence had followed me through life.

As I lie here now, extremely conscious that every breath could be my last, I know that my years in the classroom were good years. The war years were not good years. A thousand years of teaching could not erase the war from my record, but I hope what I did as a teacher may at the very least add balance. My life story will say I killed people in the war; I hope it also will mention somewhere in the fine print that I was a teacher.

4 / *Marilyn and Bucky*

MARILYN CAME ABOUT mid-morning. She was a pretty woman, tall and strong, with soft auburn hair barely touched by gray and still young-looking. She was tired. She had been here, in the ICU on the sixth floor of Memorial Hospital, almost around the clock for the last two days. Her outlook was brighter today because Bucky was coming.

She stood beside the bed, studying her husband as if hoping to see some sign of life others might not have noticed. There was none. "I miss you, sweetie," she said at length. "I wish I could get you up and dressed and take you home tonight. Bucky's coming. Maybe the two of you can make up here for the Cubs games you missed and reminisce about games you've seen and even catch up on some of the locker room talk guys are supposed to do when the women aren't around."

She smiled at her own attempt at humor, thinking how unlikely it was he and Bucky ever engaged in such chatter. But then again, she recognized that after all their years together there still were cracks in her ability to understand this man. At times it seemed as if he had something inside ticking faster than anything on the outside and, intentional or not, kept her separated from him by an impenetrable fence of final resistance.

It was the war, mostly, and she'd almost given up on trying to pierce that barrier. She wished now that she had tried harder.

She sat down in a wide chair for two backed against the wall, under a window, and took a book from her handbag. The bookmark had disappeared and she fumbled through the pages until she found the place she had last stopped reading. She read only a few pages before putting the book away, walked down the hall and got a drink at a water fountain, then returned to the room and almost at once fell asleep in the chair.

It was a restless sleep and short-lived. She woke with a start when a uniformed cleaning woman opened the door and announced her coming rather loudly with the often-heard introduction, "Housekeeping!" The woman nodded politely and brushed by Marilyn to get to a trash container in the corner.

"I'm sorry to disturb you, ma'am," she said softly.

"You're not disturbing me at all. Actually, I'm glad you woke me. I didn't intend to go to sleep."

"Sometimes that's just because you need it, though. I won't be long."

The woman went about her chores quickly, moving around quietly as if worried she might wake the patient in the middle of the room. She smiled and excused her-self again when she had finished, and quickly slipped out the door.

Marilyn stood, and once again moved close beside the bed.

"Well, sweet man," she said, speaking barely above a whisper, "we have put in some tough miles together. You've taken a few blows that would have knocked most of us down and out. I've just been along for the ride. But I want you to know, you've always left me proud and happy and I can't even imagine making the trip along-side anyone else but you."

She turned back, facing the window, and began to cry. She looked out over the tops of lesser buildings and studied the cloudless sky as if it were something new and different, a thing she hadn't seen before, and it occurred to her that she had been completely oblivious to weather and other mundane elements of her surroundings from the instant she received a call informing her of her hus-band's accident. She could barely remember what came after that. She had made calls, of course, but the only thing that had mattered was getting to his side and she had dropped everything else.

Now she was here, and she felt helpless and without hope. She could not lift him up, she could not ease his pain. She had no reason to believe he could see her or hear her or that he was in any sense aware of her pres-ence. The only indication there was life in his body came through the anemic electronic impulses displayed by the instruments above his head. She had not moved when Bucky came.

She turned to meet him, and Bucky pulled her close in a suffocating embrace. They stood that way for a long time before he pushed her back, at arms' length, and looked into her face.

"I have missed you guys so much," he said. "I'm so sorry, Marilyn. Is it as bad as you made it sound?"

"He doesn't have much of a chance. His doctor told me that from the beginning, in so many words. He didn't say it directly, but his meaning was clear. I think I'm supposed to get an update today."

Bucky stepped close beside the bed and put a hand on the patient's arm, encased in a hard cast. He stood silently for a moment, looking down on his motionless friend and shaking his head. "I can't believe it," he said then. "It hurts me to see him lying there like this and know there's nothing we can do. Damn it, it's just not fair! Do you know anything about the accident? What caused it, or how many people were hurt, or anything like that?"

"I don't know much. I think it was a construction zone or something, but nobody has told me much of anything. They said I'd eventually get a report from the state police."

"How are you holding up? You look awful tired. Are you getting any sleep?"

"Sleep? Explain the concept."

"You've got to take care of yourself, Marilyn. How about food? Did you have breakfast?"

"Coffee and a donut. About like I usually have."

Bucky shook his head. "Why do I worry about you? Marilyn will always be Marilyn and Marilyn is the toughest cookie I know. Coffee and a donut sound pretty good right now, actually. Is there someplace close I could get some?"

"There's a coffee shop right downstairs. We can go down there after a while if you'd like." She hugged him again, pulled him tight against her and lay her face down on his shoulder. "I've missed you, too. I'm glad you're here. He was so very much looking forward to this trip, Bucky."

"And so was I. I was about ready to come down there when he called and said he was coming. What is it he calls it? Down in the Shawnee?"

"Yes. He loves to say that. We're right on the south edge of the Shawnee National Forest."

"He always had a thing for trees. It really worried me that the move might not work out, but from what I can tell he seems to be pretty contented down there. It evidently turned out to be good for him, but how about you?"

Marilyn hesitated. "I hated it at first," she told him. "But he found so much peace, surrounded by forest. He said it was almost a dream come true for him. And I came to grips with it pretty quick, too. It's a good place to live. I've learned to like it very much."

Bucky looked around the room. "Seems like a decent place, if you have to be in a hospital," he said. "They apparently have a busy emergency room and I saw a helicopter ambulance on the roof over there. And it sprawls all over two or three blocks, from what I saw trying to find my way in here."

"It's a teaching hospital, as I understand it. He's had a bunch of different specialists. Doctor Morrison is his main doctor. He's the tall one with white hair if you happen to see him. And of course you have all the medical students or interns or whatever. There are so many of them I think they surely must get in each other's way sometimes."

"Heard from the kids?"

"Annie should be here soon."

"What about Craig?"

"Craig, the wanderer? The Alaskan gold prospector? Our adult son who still thinks he's a boy with no responsibilities and can just take off whenever he chooses and go wherever he likes and call his mother if he gets around to it but doesn't make it a priority because he really doesn't want to be bothered with it? Do you mean *that* Craig?"

"You have an acid tongue, Marilyn! Yes, that Craig, bag of gold and all."

Marilyn smiled. "I try to keep up a tough front on the outside because I'm such a pushover on the inside. You know Craig's in Alaska. I sent him a text message, but I've not heard anything back yet."

"Are you sure he got it?"

"I'm never sure about anything with these damned cell phones. I hate mine, but I always have it with me. I think I would have got some indication if his message didn't go through. I think he's in the middle of nowhere, but you know Craig. He'll get down here, one way or another."

Bucky stood and stretched. "We're going to be here for a while. I need to see if I can walk out some kinks after the drive. Maybe I'll go down and try those donuts. Want to come?"

"No, but you go on. I'll be down in a bit."

Bucky was barely out of the room when a fluid bag draining into the patient's arm went dry and set off an alarm. Jan rushed in and replaced it and entered a note reporting the exchange on the bedside computer.

"Is there anything new?" Marilyn asked.

"Not really." Jan turned to face her. "Everything is pretty much the same as it has been for the last several hours now. How are you holding up?"

"I'm okay. Thank you for taking care of him. My aunt is a nurse and she always says nurses do all the work and doctors get all the credit."

Jan laughed. "Oh, yeah. There's a whole lot of truth in that. He has a good one, though. Doctor Morrison is one of the best. Are you staying in town for a while?"

"I'm in a motel just down the street. It's about all I could ask in a home away from home. Do you live here in town?"

"Yep. Only about four miles away. We need a bigger house, now that the kids are growing up so fast, but I don't want to be any farther from the hospital and have a long commute in a winter blizzard."

"How old are your kids?"

"Daughter's thirteen and two boys ten and eight, all three growing like weeds."

Marilyn was stimulated by the conversation. Until Bucky came, she had felt as if she were trapped in solitude.

"I miss all the stories about kids since we moved out of the city," she said. "We have nice neighbors, but they are all older and there don't seem to be any kids on the street. But we raised a son and a daughter and I know what you can go through with them."

"Well, if you've been there you understand. I love my kids to death, but some days I'd be glad to trade them all in for puppies."

"Or kittens! But then you miss them like crazy when they grow up and leave the nest. Raising our kids is the most important thing we do, and by the time we learn how to do it right it's too late. We don't get but one time around."

"Spoken like a true mother," Jan said, as she finished adding to the computer her notes on the patient's newest vital signs. "But then if we're lucky we get to be grandmothers down the line, and I hear that's a whole lot better."

Jan left the room and Marilyn was once more alone. She thought about her children and the good years in Chicago while the young family was still together. How could time have flown by so fast? She wanted Annie and Craig here at her side, the three of them standing watch together.

Having the kids grow up and leave the nest permanently had been stressful in its own way, but this was a progressive sequence of things, stretching out over time and allowing for periods of adjustment. Selling the home in Chicago and moving to a new and vastly different region had been an *event*, sudden and unsettling. She didn't want to do it, but her husband wanted it so much she felt obligated to pretend support and actually had come to terms with the move sooner and easier than she had expected. But now her husband lay dying, her children were not here, and the family circle seemed terribly broken.

She wanted Bucky's company. She was about to pick up her handbag when she heard her phone, playing the merry tune she had chosen as a ringtone. Even though muffled inside the bag, the sound was out of place here in this somber setting, like the sudden wail of a siren in the serene hours of quiet darkness just before dawn. She fumbled through the contents of her bag and retrieved the instrument. Annie was calling.

5 / *I am*

I'M TRYING HARD NOT to give up hope. I am still here. And I am thinking clearly now. And like the French philosopher said, "I think, therefore I am." Descartes. I even remembered the name. If I can think, I exist. I am still alive. I survived the war and I have made it this far when I probably should not have come out of the wreck alive. And I know who I am.

Marilyn says we all get more chances than we deserve. I think she may be right. My life story may not be much, but it is what it is and I won't pretend to be anything I'm not. I won't deny the things I'm guilty of. I have not earned another chance and I am prepared to die, but if I should beat the odds and pull through this I will do my best to make up for the wrongs I've done. That's a promise.

You don't care about any of this, but if I can reconstruct my life story in my own mind it means I still am capable of logical thinking. And if I can occupy my brain this way, maybe it will help me avoid falling into those whirlpools of confusion that leave me discouraged almost to the point of giving up. I cannot resurrect my physical body and get up and walk, but I still must fight further loss of my mental capacity and I will.

And who knows? One day I may again walk in the woods and stroll with Marilyn among Yeats' silver apples of the moon and golden apples of the sun. These simple things, which we very much take for granted when we're able, become precious memories when we lose them. I want to reclaim them and, though I know my chances may be slight, I will struggle for this with my last ounce of energy.

My insignificant life story begins with the fact that I am a Hoosier. Yes, I know, this sounds like the punch line in a joke or something, but here they know exactly what it means. It means I'm from Indiana. I don't intend to imply that people here go around talking about Hoosiers all the time, but the Indiana state line probably is no more than forty miles to the east so the label is not strange.

I don't know whether being a Hoosier means anything else or not. Uncle Dick probably could have told me, but it didn't seem important and I never asked.

I spent the first eighteen years of my life in a little town near the Ohio River in southern Indiana, just upstream from Louisville, Kentucky, and on Uncle Dick's nearby farm. It wasn't much of a place to be from, but when I look back on it now I realize it probably was a good place to grow up.

I joined the Army as soon as I finished high school because there was nothing else to do and I wanted to see the great big world I'd only dreamed about. This wasn't a hard choice; soldiers in uniform were heroes, important, something I never had been. Joining would make my mother proud.

I got to see the world, but it turned out to be an ugly world, far worse than anything I could have anticipated. And I did not come home a hero.

I don't know, but I hope that if I could go back now and see the same world again I could find some beauty there. Maybe not much, but there always is something good if you look hard enough. The evil things men did so overwhelmed that world then that beauty seemed un-imaginable, but I'm willing to give it a second chance.

I was young and strong when I got hit in the war and that helped me survive. I'm old now and this may dimin-ish my odds of getting through this one. I don't know how old I am. I think I was born in 1949, but I can't remember what year it is now. In a new century, yes, but I can't seem to come up with precise details like dates. I know I didn't quit teaching because I was old. I quit because Marilyn said we could retire and have more time to ourselves and this is something we both wanted. Moving away from the city was something we decided on later.

Being a Hoosier really has nothing to do with who I am, of course. It is not part of how I see myself or how others see me. And the only one who ever called me a Hoosier, as far as I can remember, was a sadistic drill sergeant we had in basic combat infantry training at Fort Leonard Wood, Missouri, after I joined the Army. He never called me by name, but acted like he took pleasure in calling out "that damned Hoosier" when we were in formation and doing his best to humiliate me in front of all the other men. I suspect he had a hard time with some of the names, especially anything not strictly Anglo-Saxon and easy, and looked for simple names and other tags he could remember in calling guys out. If there was anybody else from Indiana in our company I never heard about it.

I'm proud to tell you, that drill sergeant never got me down. I think he knew in the end I had taken everything he could dish out and maybe even respected me for it. He was brutal to some extent, but I think part of this was only a tough act he thought he had to put on to do his job. This attitude was pretty common among the training cadre, but he was more crude and seemed to get mad faster.

I hated the drill sergeants then, but I see things a lot different now. They had a lot to deal with, and I think most of them took their responsibilities seriously. They understood that we could be going into combat in a matter of weeks and what we learned in training might be the difference between life and death. Whatever they might think of us individually, they wore the uniform of the U. S. Army and understood that we did the same.

And let me make a point here: Bitter as I am about the war, I still feel some pride in having worn that uniform and served my country. It's what I did in the war that stains my record, not the mere fact that I was there. Some people still do not understand this. Soldiers are individuals, like everyone else. Just because they wear the same uniform doesn't mean they are all alike. All dogs have teeth but they don't all bite.

But back to the drill sergeants, there was a serious limit to what they could do. Unless they had been in a war like the one we were thrown into, they never could have understood how day after day in combat wears on the mind as well as the body and leads men to cease to care if they ever get out alive. They couldn't have known the fatalism that eventually takes control, leaving you to no longer worry about what lies beyond the next patch of bamboo or just over the next hill but view a body bag almost with envy as the ultimate ticket home.

Maybe some of them had been there and experienced these things. Most of them probably were career soldiers and Vietnam went on for a long time. But even if they had, knowing how this war tore at men's moral fiber and teaching this to green recruits are two different things. They faced a near impossible task, in my opinion, no matter how hard they tried.

I'll grant you the military teaching method—by the numbers—is pretty effective. It's kind of like teaching you electricity by starting with how you turn on a light switch. They tried to teach us to kill instead of being killed. This means everything from how to fight another man physically, hand to hand, to how to use the weapons at your disposal. And those weapons are good for exactly what they were designed for. Their only purpose is to help you kill other human beings.

When I think back on it now, I realize something I never thought of before. The big lie in military training, the con game those instructors played, is pretty simple. They make you think you're ready for war and you're not.

The drill sergeants knew where most of us would end up. The rocky slopes of Fort Leonard Wood actually are not too different from the hills of Vietnam, but I never saw action in the hills. There was nothing where we trained that was anything like the swamps and jungles I saw. And it probably didn't matter. A few weeks of training, whether in the Ozark Mountains of Missouri or the craters of the moon, won't make you ready for real war. Nothing will.

I liked and admired the young lieutenant who was the company commander of my training unit. I think this slot should have been filled by a captain, but maybe standards weren't the same in training camp. Anyway, Lieutenant Pinchuck was a recent University of Georgia graduate who had a great sense of humor and was very even-handed in his approach to new recruits. There were a lot of times during the war when I thought about him and wished he was there in command. I don't think Lieutenant Pinchuck would have let innocents be killed.

I'm struggling to keep my mind focused. The inside of my head is the only part of my body that I seem to have any control over, and I'm afraid I don't have much control over it.

Simply telling you what I've done in my life should be the easiest challenge I can come up with. I guess it's a normal part of logical thinking that this leads you off into different directions as you go along. I've always found that true, and in most cases I don't think it's a problem. It won't hurt if I skip around a little and maybe don't get things in exactly the right order. Nobody is going to be taking notes, like they were planning to write a book about me. This is good. No book about me ever could have a happy ending.

6 / *Marilyn and Bucky*

MARILYN TOOK an elevator to the ground floor and went to the coffee shop, where she found Bucky sitting at a small table for two in a corner of the room. He greeted her with his familiar smile, and stood and pulled out the second chair and motioned for her to sit.

"Take a load off your feet and let me get you some coffee and a couple of donuts," he said.

"Have you been waiting for me? I wasn't sure how we left things."

"You just said you'd come down sooner or later. This is a pleasant enough place to just sit and relax and the coffee's good, but I'm glad you're here."

Marilyn welcomed company as much as she ever had in her entire life. The strain of all the hours spent at her husband's bedside without hope, nearly sleepless nights in a motel nearby, and paying little attention to her need for food and drink were beginning to take their toll. She was bone-tired and discouraged and she would have welcomed Jack the Ripper as a table mate as long as he was someone to talk to. But she was especially grateful that it was Bucky.

She waved off his offer to get her something, went to the counter and got a cup of black coffee and a cinnamon roll, and rejoined him at the table.

"I'm worried about you," he said, as she settled into her chair. "Have you been taking care of yourself at all? Do you want me to try to call Annie and Craig and see what's going on with them?"

"Annie's coming today. She just called."

"Thank God. I don't want you here by yourself any longer. And I'm going to come back tomorrow and stay as long as I can be of any help at all. They won't miss me at work and there's nothing on my schedule now except you."

"You're a sweetheart, Bucky. We'll get through this, however long it takes. But he's not going to make it, I think you know."

Bucky put his hand on hers. "I won't give up hope," he said. "That's a tough man you got up there. I don't believe in miracles, but—"

"No, there is not going to be any miracle. I know you're trying to give me some hope, but I've accepted this. It's only a matter of time. Doctor Morrison is not going to tell me anything different today."

"Oh, damn it, Marilyn, I know. I'm just having a hard time with it, myself. Nobody is ready for something like this, hitting us out of the clear blue like it did."

They stopped talking, as if accepting the fact that there was nothing more to be said. Marilyn took a long drink of coffee and poked at her roll with a fork. Bucky gazed across the room, out through the glassed front of the coffee shop into the busy hallway. As he turned back toward her, Marilyn looked up.

"I just realized what you said. You are working? I thought you retired."

"Yeah, I tried it. Sitting around by myself got pretty boring after a while, though. I was fortunate they were willing to take me back."

"You're looking good, Bucky. You've put on some weight. That wouldn't be a compliment to most people, but you needed it."

The expression on Bucky's face showed his pleasure. "I thought you didn't notice. Yeah, I've added about fifteen pounds since you guys moved. I worked at it. I was down to skin and bone. But you know that."

"You may be the only person I know who had to work at gaining weight. Most of us have to work to keep it off. I'm going to need some more coffee. Want some?"

Bucky agreed not only to another cup of coffee but also wanted another donut. He pushed his chair back and stood. He looked fit, now that he'd added weight, and younger than his age. He walked with a slight limp, but Marilyn thought even this had improved. She wondered whether he had been working to correct this, too, although it had been much less pronounced in recent years for reasons Bucky himself could not explain. In the early years after the war he often had needed a walking cane.

They were quickly served at the counter, returned to the table and settled into their chairs again.

"Get back to Indianapolis any?" Bucky asked. "I have some clients there now."

"Not since we moved. You may remember, we went to visit Sissy a month or so before that. We hadn't seen her in a long time. He always said he didn't want to lose touch with her and I think he enjoyed our brief visit."

"I'd forgotten she lives in Indy. And Geri is still in California?"

"Yes. San Diego. It had been at least three or four years since we talked to her, before I called her about the accident. I hate to say it, but you know I don't think she even cared. I think Sissy will try to come, though."

"I don't think I ever met Geri."

Marilyn stared into her coffee cup, as if examining the contents. She still looked down when she spoke. "I hate to say it, Bucky, because she's family. But Geri is a miserable excuse for a human being. You would never think she came out of the same family as he and Sissy. I liked her well enough when we first got married, but she changed over the years."

"It happens."

"I always liked Sissy and his mother. Not that I ever saw much of either one. His mother worked all the time, even after she got old enough to retire. And you know, I don't think he really knew his mother very well. And of course he barely remembered his father."

"Uncle Dick took the place of his father."

Marilyn laughed. "Uncle Dick was a character," she said. "But that old man loved him, no doubt about that. While he was a boy, anyway. It always seemed strange to me that they never really were close again after he left home. Uncle Dick didn't even come to our wedding."

"Something happened between them. I never knew exactly what it was. I think it had something to do with the war, though."

"Which war? Uncle Dick's or his?"

"His. I knew when they had their falling out, but he never told me what it was all about. The war messed us up in so many ways, Marilyn. Maybe it changed him in ways Uncle Dick didn't like. We'll never know, now."

Bucky was about to say more, but Marilyn suddenly interrupted. She spoke rather urgently, as if at this very instant she had thought of something important.

"Did you really use peyote? I remember him telling me once you did, but he didn't want to talk about it and I didn't push him. I think it only came up in reference to Indianapolis some way."

Bucky laughed. "Yes, we did, and I'm sure he remembered the experience well enough to tell you about it if he wanted to. Peyote is a different animal."

"I've never done drugs, so I wouldn't know."

"Peyote is an hallucinogen. I guess it's the kind of thing true druggies have in mind when they talk about 'tripping.' Maybe they get used to it, but man, it took us on a trip I wouldn't want to go on again."

Marilyn's interest had been roused. "This is going to sound foolish, Bucky," she said, "but I'd like for you to tell me about it. I have so many regrets about the things he and I never talked about. Mostly it was the war, but he never told me much about those early days in Terre Haute, either. Before I came along, I mean. I know you guys had some rough times. I've always wished I could have been part of them. Maybe I could have helped."

"You did help. He pulled out of it only because of you. You're feeling guilty over something that certainly wasn't your fault."

"You probably are right. It's just that I wish now I had heard all the stories he never told. The war and those dark days after it were so much a part of his life, and he never shared them. What I'm feeling guilty about is not helping him get over all that. Maybe—"

"He was ashamed of it. I think you were the first truly beautiful thing that ever came along in his life. Well, except for his poetry. He didn't want to drag you down in the gutter where we'd been."

"You understood him so very well, Bucky. But would you just tell me about the peyote? I think it was so different he thought of it as some sort of an adventure, separate from all the rest. I think he wanted to tell me about it but never quite got up the nerve."

Bucky pulled himself up in his chair, holding onto the edges of the table. "Yeah, it was an adventure, I guess. We didn't know what we were getting into," he said. "One night we were having an unusually hard time and he wanted to go to Indianapolis and look for some strong stuff. The demons he carried from the war were a lot worse than mine, as you know, and I was afraid he was about to go over the edge. Anyway, we hit the usual corner in Indy and a punk selling just about anything anyone could want offered cactus buttons—"

"Wait, wait. I don't know what that means."

"Sorry. It's one of the forms peyote comes in. I think it's just little chunks they cut off the cactus and dry, so it's like little pills. You chew them. Tastes awful, but kicks in pretty quick. I guess it affects different people in different ways, but we both thought we were floating in the air. It made me feel great, but he got all sad and started crying about the war and said he could see the music coming from a bar on the corner."

"*See* music? Really?"

"That's what he said. He could see the music, and it was all in bright colors. We were totally out of it, Marilyn. We spent the night on the streets of Indy and thought we had died and gone to heaven or something. He was having hallucinations like crazy. At one point he started reciting Tennyson poetry and went on until he couldn't think of any more. And there's no telling what all we did that we didn't remember in the morning."

Marilyn shook her head sadly. "I just wish I had been there for him."

"No," Bucky said, "on this night be glad you weren't. He was off on another planet. We both were. And, oh, I do remember one more thing. Somewhere along the way he thought he was in Aunt Nell's garden looking at the flowers. He got all upset then over one of her little statues being broken. He was afraid she was going to think it was his fault."

"Aunt Nell gave him a hard time. But thank you for telling me all this. I should have heard it from him."

They sat in the coffee shop for another hour, making small talk about things that had nothing to do with war or husbands or sisters or best friends or accidents or injuries or anything unpleasant. Weather forecasts on a large-screen television set mounted high on a wall across the room absorbed a portion of this time and led to a discussion of the high temperatures. Bucky asked about southern Illinois scenic and recreation areas he'd heard about and Marilyn told him about the Garden of the Gods and the River-to-River Trail that crossed the Shawnee National Forest from the Ohio to the Mississippi.

"And you really have mountains down there?"

She laughed. "Hard to see them as mountains, but pretty nice hills. Yeah, the Illinois Ozarks. Who knew?"

"And he's happier there, with the forest and all?"

Marilyn's eyes swelled with tears. "Yes, he's happier there. I believe this was something he needed."

Bucky's expression was demanding, his brow arched and his eyes fixed on her face. "You've been a good wife, Marilyn," he said, his voice firm. "I know it hasn't been easy. But he's lucky to have you and he would be the first to say so. And Craig and Annie know what you did for him, turning your own life upside down in hopes a move would help him find peace. Just ask Annie when she gets here."

"I hope you're right," she answered, a hint of doubt in her tone. "Annie has been on the outs with him for a while now, and may not know how much he's enjoyed life in the woods. But maybe they've had more contact than I think they have. I suppose we will find out soon enough."

"I'm glad she's coming, Marilyn. You need her as much as he does."

Marilyn smiled. This was in some part because she looked forward to seeing Annie, but more than anything else she smiled because it was Bucky seated across the table. Bucky always had it within him to make life better.

7 / *I look back*

I DO NOT KNOW what goes on around me and not being able to communicate what I think I feel is like being trapped in my own special hell. I'm on my own. If I am to have any chance at all, I must save myself. My brain is still functioning. I am alive. I can do this. No matter that I have failed others so many times, now I must not fail myself.

I'm looking back at everything in the rear-view mirror, so to speak, and now I understand there were things that affected me the rest of my life and therefore were far more important than I knew at the time. Those first few months in the Army gave me a much wider view of the world. Basic combat infantry training is an intense period when you exist in an extremely close relationship with a small group of other human beings you never saw before and don't expect ever to see again. The Army introduced me to a lot of guys from backgrounds much different from mine.

I developed an intense camaraderie with these men during this period, which I recall now with a great deal of satisfaction. I was part of something new to me, something I never had experienced or even thought possible. I was part of a team now, no longer merely an insignificant inhabitant of a small corner of my very limited world.

I was a soldier in the United States Army! I had common purpose with these men and all the others who wore this uniform and for the first time in my life I could see my future as an integral part of something much greater than I. All this brought me a sense of contentment I never had felt before.

And my team went to war. The war played such an immense role in making me who I am that I tend to divide my life story into two parts: before the war and after. Much of the pre-war part centers around Uncle Dick.

The only advice I got from Uncle Dick when I was about to leave home—forever, as it turned out—was, "Don't let them get you down, son." He assured me I could take everything they could dish out and come through standing tall. I wish I had told him about the Hoosier treatment I got from that drill sergeant at Fort Leonard Wood, but I never did. He would have been proud of me for handling it the way I did.

He remembered his own Army experiences pretty well, but from things he told me his war was not the same as mine. Even so, it still seems to me he should have understood things I told him when I came home that I had been afraid to tell anyone else. He didn't. I'm sorry I ever thought he would.

Uncle Dick was my great uncle, my grandmother's brother, and the only man who had much influence on me when I was a child. He was a good old man who tried to be fun to be around and I know he really cared about me. I loved him very much.

He hardly ever talked about himself, but I know he was proud of his and Grandmama's heritage, claiming family roots in Virginia, and he liked to say he was only a weary traveler on "the road of life." I don't think he ever went to church but he referred to "the good Lord" a lot and I believe he was religious in his own way. I don't recall him ever mentioning his father.

Like all of us, Uncle Dick had his faults. He carried the ignorance and prejudices typical of his time, no doubt, including what I recognize now as an obvious bent toward racism.

"The birds don't jazz one another," he proclaimed one day, and I guess he could tell I didn't understand his point. "Look at it this way, boy. You've got your blue jays and your cardinals. Have you seen any purple birds lately? The good Lord did not intend for the colors to mix."

I wish I could go back now and argue the point. Uncle Dick respected a good debate, as long as you could tell him reasons for your position and not just insist he accept your opinion. I'd tell him how birds are primitive animals that operate on instinct and not feelings and emotions and that's why humans are more advanced. And then I'd say Nita had mixed blood and was beautiful, but then I'd have to think it through and admit that maybe feelings and emotions aren't always so good after all. Anyway, when I think about birds I think about flying and what a wondrous thing this would be. William Blake may have put it best: "No bird soars too high, if he soars with his own wings." I don't think Blake worried about a bird's color, either.

I know. I'm about to go off on a tangent here. I want to keep my thinking on track. That's what I need to do, my self-imposed test. So I was talking about Uncle Dick's racism.

It was easy to dismiss, because race relations weren't a big issue in our region in those days. There weren't many black residents, and I doubt Uncle Dick ever knew a black person well. There were only two black students in my high school and they lived on the far side of the county somewhere.

Marilyn says some of the small towns in southern Illinois around where we live now used to have so-called sundown laws, that black people weren't allowed there after sundown. I remember Professor Sampson talking about sundown laws when I was in college. He said the problems caused by racial prejudice in America never were limited to the South, although of course nothing else came close to the ultimate prejudice of thinking it was okay for people of one race to hold people of another race as slaves and there is a big difference between social segregation and legal segregation as official policy.

If I haven't mentioned Professor Sampson before, he was my favorite teacher at Indiana State. He told us about the Greenwood Massacre in Tulsa and the ugly race riots in East St. Louis in more modern times than the Civil War and how these and other ugly incidents of racial prejudice and ignorance have been largely ignored in the history books. This would have bothered me if I had decided to be a history teacher, but for the most part teaching poetry is like teaching love and beauty. I don't think anyone would disagree that we need more of these.

It's a mark of his effectiveness as a teacher that I remember so much of what Professor Sampson said. He tended to put things into broader context, so that you understood why they were important. He talked a lot about how we treated the American Indians, too, and I never could have imagined then that one day I'd live almost within a baseball throw of a branch of the Trail of Tears where the Cherokee and other Native American tribes struggled across southern Illinois on their forced march from the East to the Indian Territory in the 1830s. Marilyn says it runs somewhere right behind our house.

Professor Sampson told us that throughout history there is a common thread of human beings trying to make other human beings *different* in order to feel superior. I thought about how they told us in the war to go out and kill "gooks" like this was justified, and then I suddenly had raw mental images of bloody bodies and got sick and had to leave class. I wish now I had told him why. He encouraged students to take part in discussion, and he would have understood about "gooks."

And I remember he told us more people have been killed in wars over religion than most other causes, and if I were in his class today I'd ask if wars over love and beauty also might merit consideration. Homer said there was no reason to blame the Trojans that they "long suffer woes" for such a woman as Helen. But maybe I'm just looking for a self-serving excuse to use the words of a poet again. I can't help it that Homer said things so much better than I can.

Professor Sampson was a great teacher. His classes were popular and hard to get into. I tried to be like him when I started teaching, but I know I fell far short.

I was talking about Uncle Dick, though, and I need to get back on track. Uncle Dick's prejudices had something of a soft edge. He and my grandmother shared a library of a few old classics, books handed down to them by their mother. He wanted to make sure Grandmama read more than her beloved Tennyson poems to me, and he read to me from *Uncle Tom's Cabin*, *Tom Sawyer*, and *Huckleberry Finn*.

Uncle Dick was very fond of the passage in *Uncle Tom's Cabin* about Eliza's treacherous crossing of the frozen Ohio River ice floe, and read it to me several times. I don't know if he liked it so much because it was exciting or only because it was about the river he loved and not the story itself. He read to me about Tom Sawyer and Huckleberry Finn, too, and claimed Mark Twain actually was jealous that he lived in Missouri and had to write about the Mississippi when he really wished he could live on the mighty Ohio.

He always stressed his opinion that, of the two, the Ohio was much more important. Until they join down at Cairo, he insisted, the Ohio River is wider than the Mississippi and "settlers coming down the Ohio had a lot more to do with the history of this great nation than anybody trying to get up the Mississippi." But he still loved to read to me from Mark Twain.

I remembered all this when we moved south from Chicago and early on I drove down to Cairo and walked right to the edge of the water at the confluence of these two great rivers. Uncle Dick was right, the Ohio is wider. And I remembered how he said he wished he could kneel down at this very spot some day and dip one hand in the Mississippi and the other in the Ohio and I did exactly that, in his honor. It would have been nice to have him there beside me.

It was a marvelous feeling, standing where the two rivers come together and thinking about their respective roles in American history. I knew I owed this all to Uncle Dick.

I want to live to take the grandchildren there. They may not know about Tom Sawyer and Huckleberry Finn nor Eliza and Uncle Tom, and they haven't had an Uncle Dick to read to them from Mark Twain and Harriet Beecher Stowe. They won't understand the historical importance of the site. But I believe they will have fun watching all the barge tows moving up and down the rivers.

Marilyn thinks this is a good idea, too. She says this would be a good geography lesson for them. I doubt that they know geography the way I did when I was a kid making up stories about my father, but they still might be impressed that they can stand in one state and look up at bridges that cross into two others.

I guess Uncle Dick's boyhood was a lot like mine. Stories about the rivers were of exaggerated importance to him because his world was very limited. The Ohio River was something he knew, something he identified with. He spent a great part of his life on its bank.

And like me, Uncle Dick saw an expanded universe only when he went to war. He did not visit France as a tourist, but as a United States Army soldier. There ought to be a better way.

8 / *Jan, Kendra, and Marty*

JAN WAS NOT ESPECIALLY eager to get back to the nurses' station at the end of the hall after she finished her early morning rounds, but hurried anyway. Rushing was an ingrained habit. In her entire time at Memorial Hospital, there had been few days when she didn't have a patient in every bed on her floor. The ICU was not much different. There were two empty beds today, but she had little doubt they would be filled before the end of her shift and new patients often were the most difficult.

She stepped behind the counter that surrounded the nurses' station on three sides, poured out some cold coffee, and refilled her cup from a freshly brewed pot and added artificial sweetener and creamer. The two nurses already there hardly looked up.

"You guys are kind of quiet this morning," Jan said. "Anybody got anything exciting to report on?"

"We were just waiting for you," Marty said. "Kendra was sure you'd have something exciting to talk about. We've been nearly breathless in anticipation. Now don't tell us you're going to let us down!"

"Hey, there are not many things in life that are certain, but one sure thing is that I am always the last one to know what's going on. Excitement and me don't even have a nodding acquaintance."

"How's that accident patient this morning?" Kendra asked. "I thought he wasn't expected to last through the night."

"Pretty much hopeless. It'll be a miracle if he makes it."

"Well," Marty declared, "my grandmother says that miracles happen all around us. She says we're all just too busy with our own self-interests to notice. When does Phil get home?"

"He'll be back Friday, all worn out from the stupid drills the Guard runs them through. He eats this stuff up, but I don't know why. It still just seems to me like grown men playing kids' war games with real guns. They actually take their tanks and light artillery and all that."

"Tanks? I thought he was air."

"He is. I didn't mean his unit takes tanks. Other Guard units do, though. He says they throw everybody together and try to make it feel like the real thing. You know, stage phony attacks and all that."

"Well, it'd be real enough for me. But I'll bet he comes back horny as hell after being gone so long. You guys will have a lot of catching up to do, right? I wouldn't mind if Mitch had something to go away a couple of weeks for. He might appreciate me a little more if he had to go without for a while."

"You mean you guys don't go at it every night like newlyweds anymore?"

"I wish! Sometimes I think that law office is more important than I am, especially right now. He's working on some kind of investigation for the state. Half the time he doesn't get home till midnight."

Kendra threw up her hands. "Just leave it to Marty to make everything about sex," she said. "What we have here is a sex-crazed woman. Right, Jan?"

"If you say so. How's Kendra this morning?"

"I'm still half asleep. We stayed up too late last night watching some really stupid movie on television. We were just talking about Phil before you walked up. Marty says you're worried he's going to be sent to Afghanistan. Could that really happen?"

Jan took a careful sip of hot coffee and shook her head almost imperceptibly. "There is a rumor his unit might be sent over there," she told Kendra. "We don't know anything for sure but, yeah, I'm scared it could happen. But hey, girl, look at you! You're beginning to show!"

"I thought you'd never notice."

"Sure we noticed," Marty said. "But we just thought you'd been eating too much pizza. You have to be careful, you know. You get all excited over some woman being pregnant but you're afraid to say anything because it might be just belly fat."

"Yeah, but you already knew this is not belly fat. I told you guys way back."

"Pay no attention to her," Jan said. "Marty is just being Marty."

Marty smiled and put a hand on Kendra's shoulder. "Jan's right," she said. "You knew I was only kidding. We're really happy for you, kid. But don't worry, we will be watching over you. If it begins to look like too much pizza we'll come down on you like that tough nun in Catholic school you told us about!"

Kendra returned the smile, then took her cell phone from her purse and dialed a number. After several rings with no answer she ended the call. "Could one of you guys give me a ride home tonight?" she asked. "I've been having car trouble and I can't get an answer from the stupid garage to find out if it's going to be fixed."

"Sure," Jan told her. "I go right out your way, anyhow. What's the matter with the old Ford?"

"Who knows? About a hundred thousand too many miles. It's worn out. But I can't afford a new one. Have you heard anything about the new pay scale they keep promising us?"

Marty answered before Jan could speak. "Yeah, my grandma told me about it when I was just a little girl. She said don't count your money till they put it in your grimy little hand. We're just nurses, honey. They gotta pay the doctors and accountants and cooks and janitors and computer-fixers first. That new pay scale may not come in your lifetime."

Jan detected a momentary expression of alarm on Kendra's face. She had no desire to inject herself into her friend's personal life, but she was bothered by the prospect of Kendra having problems she had not revealed. A woman expecting her first child did not need anything else to worry about.

And neither did she. Ever since she'd first heard the rumor that her husband's Air National Guard unit might be called to active duty, the mere idea that this could happen had weighed heavily on her mind. Phil's summer encampment took him away from her and the children for longer periods of time than she was comfortable with; having him taken away for a year or more seemed a loss she could hardly conceive of. She had tried to put it out of her mind, telling herself there was no need to worry over a mere rumor. Chances were, no such action was in the works. But still, deep down, a persistent inner voice said such rumors rarely came about unless there was some basis in fact. She might very well have good reason to be afraid.

9 / *I know the shadow world*

I THINK A DOCTOR OR nurse or somebody is working over me. What could they possibly do? They probably want more blood, if I have any left to give. I tried to blink my eyes to show them I'm still alive but I couldn't make it happen. Or, if I did blink I couldn't tell. I think my eyes are closed and I can't open them, or maybe they are open and I can't tell the difference. I still see shapes sometimes, but they seem to come and go.

It would be hard to describe how I feel right now. It's something like being zonked out on drugs, or falling-down drunk. I have experienced both. The difference is, then it felt good because I wanted to close out the world and now it doesn't because I want to cry out and let the world know I'm still here but I can't move or make a sound. The world I know is spinning all around me, but I am detached from it. I feel like I am lost in a strange cosmos in which I can't trust my own senses.

Maybe I told you already, but yes, there was a time when I was little more than an ordinary street junkie. Those first months in Terre Haute weren't easy. Bucky and I both had too many ghosts. My biggest worry was how I might get my next fix. I drank a lot, too. Alcohol always made me sick, and it didn't help until I had had enough to pass out. A needle in the arm or pills or powder worked a lot faster. When I look back on that time, I remember all the nights we tried to drink our-selves into oblivion or numb our brains on cheap street drugs and I wonder how we made it.

But I also remember how Bucky carried me through the darkest hours and I appreciate something now I didn't make enough of at the time: Bucky's demons were not the same as mine. He had nothing to feel guilty for.

I'm not proud of that period in my life, which lasted through most of my first year in college. When all the hurts take hold you have to find relief. We were not particular. We scored wherever we could, with whatever we could find and I have to wonder now how we sur-vived. Bucky got us some peyote in Indianapolis one night. We didn't know what it was. I won't try to tell you what it was like, but I'll give you some advice. Don't do peyote.

Had I not found Marilyn, I doubt I would have es-caped that wasted life other than through some extra-ordinary event. I would have overdosed on cheap drugs, or maybe have been mugged and left for dead in an alley.

It is possible a life-threatening experience might have sounded alarms and brought me to my senses, but I doubt it. I didn't care enough to make the effort. Marilyn was the big difference. And Bucky helped a lot, too, and indirectly, Uncle Dick.

Bucky told me plainly I could never expect Marilyn to accept me unless we climbed our way out of the sewers. I knew he was right. And, being Bucky, he promised to help. My struggle would be his struggle.

I fell back on a simple work ethic Uncle Dick had taught me. It was a mantra he lived by that if you have a responsibility, no matter how tedious or distasteful it may be, you meet it. You show up for work every day, he told me many times, and you do your best.

I looked at myself in the mirror one morning after a night of hard drinking and saw what a disgusting person I had become. How could Marilyn or Bucky or anyone else stand to be near me? I thought about Grandmama and Uncle Dick. I'd taken responsibility for getting a college degree and I needed to show up for work every day until I'd done it. It was time to push the drugs and alcohol aside and meet my responsibilities the way Uncle Dick said.

Bucky agreed. The war wasn't going away, he said, but we had to go on with the rest of our lives and we might as well do it the best we could. That day, for the first time, we became serious about our studies. It was not easy and it didn't happen overnight. More than once, when I felt like I was making good progress, I slipped back into the old habits and had to start all over again. Bucky never let me down. He's done so much for me and all I gave him in return was betrayal.

But it was Marilyn who made the difference. She knew what was going on, and quietly encouraged me when I was at my lowest point and subtly praised me for having the courage and determination to do what I needed to do. And she did this in her usual fashion, never making an issue of it or forcing a discussion but simply being aware of and concerned about what was happening and being there when I needed her. Just Marilyn being Marilyn.

Terre Haute had something of an anti-war movement, but it didn't become a hot bed of protests. Even after the Kent State students were shot by Ohio National Guard troops there were no real eruptions like they had in some college communities. Bucky and I had mixed feelings about the protests. It was good to see that students cared about the war, but it was almost comical to see how little they understood about what it was like to be in it the way we were. They seemed to be protesting the soldiers as much as the politicians who sent them, and that was hard for Bucky to witness. It was even harder for me, but for a different reason.

Even now there is a painful residue from those long days and nights when I was in the grip of drugs and, to a lesser extent, alcohol. It's not what you might imagine. I don't fear for myself, that I might one day slide back into that wasted way of life, because I don't matter. I fear for Craig and Annie. Once they grew up and left home, their world was no longer my world and I could no longer watch over them. How can I know what stresses they face, how desperate they might become for relief from the anxieties of life? I do know the pitfalls that could await if it comes to this, and how easy it is to end up a slave to whatever brings comfort.

But I know they will not be in war. I find consolation in this, because I know it was the war that led me into that world of shadows and fear and, in the end, total indifference to my own fate.

I wish Annie would come. She may be here, but I don't think so. I will somehow sense her presence if she's anywhere near.

Marilyn drove Annie off, I think. Not intentionally. They just let a little quarrel grow into a big one, two determined women who were too proud to back down. I tried to stay out of it. And I did, for a long time. Too long, I guess. I should have got between them sooner and kept at it until they had smoothed things over and regained the relationship a mother and daughter ought to have.

Worst of all, I managed to alienate Annie, myself. And she was everything to me, still the little girl who ran after her daddy and crawled on his lap and threw her arms around his neck and clung to him like some needy waif. She still is. I'd give anything to have her arms around my neck again and have her cling to me and put her hand on my heart the way she did as a child.

I'm not sure I remember exactly what their quarrel was about. Something petty. That's easy for me to say, of course. Petty to me, but important to them. I think Annie was careless with her money and Marilyn felt it was a mother's obligation to straighten her out. Marilyn made too much of it and Annie got tired of her being preachy.

What got lost in the whole thing was that Marilyn grew up in a family as poor as church mice, where a few extra dollars a month was a luxury that didn't come along very often. What she earned as a baby sitter, from the time she was barely more than a child, herself, went into the family's food money. It couldn't have been much, but as my grandmother used to say, "If you only have a dollar a dime can look right big." A dime still looks pretty big to Marilyn, and it was hard for her to watch Annie throw away her money and not say anything.

I tried not to take a position, although I did get a bit tired of Annie complaining to me about her mother trying to run her life. I was too much of a coward to take her mother's side. I should have, but I was too unsure of myself as usual, afraid to offend my little girl. The irony is, I think that my not siding with her mother is what eventually drove Annie away. I believe she knew, deep down, that her mother was right and my cowardice ate away at her respect for me.

Daddy's little girls expect daddy to be strong. Like Sir Galahad. But I'm too conscious of Tennyson's glorious Sir Galahad portrait: "My strength is the strength of ten because my heart is pure." Pure heart? Lord Tennyson wasn't talking about me.

Whatever her feelings toward me now, though, Annie will come around. She's always been a very forgiving woman. And she tried to comfort anyone she thought was hurt, even as a little girl. I could use some of that comfort now. I would welcome her mint tea, and we'd talk about how Uncle Dick taught me to make sassafrass tea from the roots of trees and she would want to go out and find a sassafrass tree and dig roots and come home and make tea but she knew it would not be as good as her mint tea and I would agree and say no one else could make tea as good as hers. And she'd throw her arms around my neck again, and feel my heart with her little hand and the world would be at peace.

Annie always was fascinated with nature. I remember once showing her an inchworm, humping along in its funny way on a porch railing. I plucked it up and put it on her sleeve and told her now she was being measured for new clothes. That's what my grandmother always told us, and my sisters and I watched for these little caterpillars and captured them when we could, just in case this was true. Annie wrote this off as foolishness, but barraged me with questions like what did it eat and how long would it live and would it turn into a butterfly some day and didn't I think it would be wonderful to be able to fly?

I had to look up "inchworm" in an encyclopedia and show her, partly because she really wanted to know and partly because she knew I didn't know much about the subject and I wanted her to have confidence in what I told her. I read to her about metamorphosis and showed her pictures of the kind of moth the inchworm turned into and we talked about flying. In her usual style, she turned this into a discussion of angels.

With Annie, you always end up following the direction she sets rather than leading her in the direction you want to go. She got her mother's strength of character, along with her way of viewing things as they are and not being sidetracked by the way she wishes they were. And she's done well. She got a degree in biology and went on to graduate school at the University of Chicago. Now she teaches environmental science or whatever they call it at Western Michigan University.

Annie has a way of seeing through the haze and knowing when I feel down and out. She can brighten my spirits when everybody else would just wring their hands and give up on me. If I could talk to her right now, I'd tell her I feel as low as that ugly little inchworm, humping along on a porch rail or window sill and barely able to see what lies right in front of my eyes. And I know what she'd say. She would remind me that if I were an inchworm I would have wings one day soon and suddenly a vast new universe such as I never even dreamed of would open before me as I soared on my own wings above the humdrum world of the past.

She'd give me a lecture on how art imitates nature and the humanities draw on science because it is the only way we can find answers to the great dilemmas of life. I'd pretend to challenge her, and then throw in the towel and say I had no evidence to offer to prove she was wrong. She would remind me how I always said life is continuous and cite all the times I had pointed to the rebirth of trees in the spring because I was a backward child raised in the woods—a favorite joke between us—and question whether there was a parallel in man unless we allowed the spirit to count.

Annie told me once that she found the metamorphosis of the inchworm a perfect metaphor for death and resurrection, which she felt religious folk carried too far with talk of eternal life. Science and nature made more sense to her than somebody's blind faith. And I quoted Tennyson, as usual, "There lives more faith in honest doubt . . . than in half the creeds."

I'm afraid that whatever faith I had, I lost a lot of it in Vietnam. Some guys say they got religion in the war, and others say their religion was tested. The problem for me is, if there is a singular God who has the power to control the universe, how would He let war happen? I don't think there's ever been a war that didn't lead to the death and suffering of lots of innocent people.

I always felt better after discussions with Annie, simply from the pride I took in recognizing, once again, that this is my child. A man who fathered this woman could not be all bad. I hope she comes, and I hope it is soon. I don't have much confidence that there is a lot of time left. But maybe I'm just fooling myself. If she were here right now, would I really know?

I suppose if something's going on, they have not given up on me. And if the doctors still have hope, who am I to disagree? I will hold on as long as I can, and make myself believe I will see my little Annie again.

10 / *Kendra and Jan*

K ENDRA WAS QUIET AS they rode across town, which for her was unusual. Her silence reinforced Jan's worry. She tried to make idle chatter as she drove, commenting on the well-groomed lawns and children drawing with colored chalk on the sidewalks, a beautiful bed of red roses, a hedge that needed a trim, and an occasional rough patch in the pavement. Even though she knew it was a cypress, she asked Kendra what kind of tree they passed, growing in the parkway, that stood out as different from the common oaks and ash and maples and occasional large and ancient sycamores that prevailed. Kendra didn't know.

Two blocks into the familiar section of town where Kendra lived, with its modest, look-alike frame houses painted in similar earth tone colors, Jan pulled over to the curb and stopped. She turned to face her passenger. Kendra looked away.

"Okay, what's going on?" Jan said. She turned off the engine and swiveled in her seat, hoping to offer a clear indication that she was seriously concerned.

"It's nothing. Really."

"I know you better than that. You've not been this quiet in all the time I've known you. I'm your friend, Kendra. If it's none of my business just say so and I'll butt out. But I want you to know I'm here for you if you need me. And you know I don't go blabbing to everyone else."

Kendra burst into tears. "It's embarrassing, Jan. I don't know what to do."

"Do you want to talk about it?"

"No, not really. But I need to tell somebody, and you are a good friend. It's just that I know there's nothing you or anyone else can do. It's my problem and I have to deal with it."

Jan reached over and took her hand. "But you know I can listen," she said. "Sometimes that's worth a lot. And don't sell me short! No promises, but you don't know what I can do till you give me a chance. Okay?"

Kendra took a handkerchief from her purse and dabbed at her tears, then wiped her nose. She managed a smile, which Jan took as an encouraging sign. Jan gripped her friend's hand and waited expectantly.

"It's probably not what you'd think," Kendra said. "Mark's not running around on me, or anything like that."

"That's not something I would have thought, or at least it wouldn't have been the first thing."

"It is about him, though. It's . . . oh, this is so hard."

"Look. You don't have to tell me anything you don't want to. I'm here to listen when you want me to, but you won't get any pressure from me to say anything you're not comfortable to tell me. Okay?"

Kendra turned away, and looked out the car window. "I know," she said, "and it's probably going to come out sooner or later, anyway."

She turned back to face Jan, and her words spilled out in a rapid stream. "We're going broke. I just had a check bounce at the grocery store, and there should be plenty of money in the account. Mark is spending way too much, and I don't know what he's spending it on."

"Writing checks? You can't see who they are made out to?"

"Some of it goes by wire transfers, you know, electronic. And he makes checks to 'cash.' I've asked him about it and he refuses to talk about it. He actually told me it's none of my business. And that's not at all like him. He'd never say that unless something was really bothering him. I'm afraid if I try to push him it'll just make things worse."

"And you've not had money problems before? Wait, that's none of my business. I didn't mean—"

"No, no, that's all right. We have never had money problems. We have two incomes and we've always had a joint checking account and always been open with each other about money. This is all new, Jan. I just don't know what to do."

Jan felt helpless. She wanted very much to be supportive, to find the words to make Kendra feel better. But now that Kendra had opened up to her, she didn't know what to say. She was embarrassed by her own long silence.

"I'm sorry," she said finally. "I want to help, but—"

"But there's nothing you can do. I know that."

Kendra's eyes filled with tears again. Jan slid across the seat and reached out to her, taking her in a gentle embrace. They sat this way for a few minutes, without talking, Kendra sobbing softly. Then Kendra suddenly pushed her away, as if in anger.

"I'm sorry," Jan told her. "I didn't mean to—"

"I'm not mad at you. I'm mad at me. I'm behaving like a child. Hey, we're nurses. We face life and death every day, right? I'm acting like an idiot and I've dragged you into this. I'm the one who should be sorry."

Jan tried not to laugh, but couldn't help herself. Her friend's sudden and complete change in attitude struck her as funny, but she also laughed because she was relieved. Kendra with spirit and determination was the Kendra she knew. This Kendra would prevail.

"Whatever happens, I'm here for you," Jan said. "You'll get to the bottom of this. Mark's a good man. If he has problems, I'll bet he opens up to you real soon— especially once he sees you're upset and worried. He knows you carry the checkbook, and you've confronted him over this so he knows it's not a secret he can keep. I'd give him, I don't know, maybe two weeks before he asks for help."

Kendra wiped her eyes and nose again and began to laugh. "You're good," she said. "Am I going to get a bill for this? You already know my checks bounce."

"Let's just charge this one up to professional courtesy. Anyway, I want you to owe me. Next time I'll be the one who needs a shoulder to cry on."

"I do feel better, and I know you're probably right. Mark's never been one to keep things from me. Not till now. But I guess we better get on home, before somebody starts worrying about us."

Jan drove ahead for the remaining two blocks and dropped Kendra off, feeling better for having made an effort to help. Being open about her feelings was not one of her own personal characteristics, but she knew from their several years of close friendship that Kendra generally tended to be much more forthcoming.

Or was she merely rationalizing?

Maybe I pushed her too hard, she thought. *Would I have been willing to tell her about it if I had been the one with such a problem?*

She knew the answer. Although she understood the importance of sharing feelings instead of keeping everything bottled up inside when she was worried or depressed, she never would have revealed a similar concern to one of her co-workers.

Phil's mother, who regularly stayed with the kids during the day, had dinner almost ready when Jan got home. The kids all seemed to be in good humor and the house was calm. But there was an empty place at the table. A few minutes into the meal, Emmie stopped eating and looked her mother directly in the eye. Jan knew the expression on her daughter's face. It was one of apprehension, coalescing with Emmie's usual determination.

"Mom, is Daddy *ever* going to get home?" Emmie demanded. "It seems like he must have been gone for a month already."

"I know," her mother told her. "It does seem like a long time. But he should be home in three days if all goes according to schedule."

"I hope so. I just worry the Guard will find some way to mess things up."

Jan suddenly felt very much alone, even here at the dinner table among family. She missed her husband very much. He was the one she came home to, as much as to the children, and she was overwhelmed by his absence. Now, she was the one who needed very much to talk. She longed for Phil's presence and desperately wished she could discuss Kendra's problem with him. She would take comfort in sharing her apprehension with her soulmate and best friend and find release from her own pressing anxiety. He would sympathize and offer sound advice. And then, tomorrow, she would pass his words along to Kendra, giving her friend new hope. He would be home soon, but she needed and wanted him now.

11 / *I wish I could believe*

I KEEP GOING INTO and coming out of periods of darkness, and I don't know how long they last. It's like a day when the sun is bright for a time and then dimmed as a cloud passes over and then really bright again. The difference is, this cloud cover leaves me in total darkness. "Black as your cellar's midnight," as that famous newsman said. I don't remember his name but I remember he always smoked cigarettes on television.

I am in a period of light just now. Even though my thinking may be a little fuzzy, I'm very much aware of who I am and I know what happened to me. After the war, I mean.

When I come out of the dark spells, I feel like I've been asleep and dreaming. I usually don't remember the dreams, but they seem to register with my brain so that the focus already is fixed when I become conscious of what's going on in my head. It is as if the topic already is set and I have no choice but to go along with it. Much too often it has something to do with the war, and when it has to do with the war it usually involves people dying.

This time, the topic is Marilyn. If I dreamed of her it was a beautiful dream and I truly am sorry I don't remember it. She makes dreams beautiful.

While I recall very few other things as vividly as I do those that happened in the war, one event that easily rates this distinction is the first time I saw her. She was the prettiest thing I'd ever seen. My first thought was that she might have been the model for Tennyson's Lady of Shalott, "A daughter of the gods, divinely tall, And most divinely fair." This single beautiful memory balances a lot of ugly ones.

I've heard it said that good things happen to good people. This is my testimony that good things happen to not-so-good people, too. People like me.

After struggling through but somehow surviving a year of college in Terre Haute, I signed up for a couple of summer semester classes to speed up graduation so I could get a job and earn my way. Marilyn and I ended up in an early morning English literature class together. Yeats said love comes in at the eye, and I think I was in love with her almost from the instant I walked into that classroom and saw her sitting there on the front row

There was a vacant seat next to hers, even though most of those in the room were taken. Looking back, I could almost believe what happened that day shows there really is a divine plan for the universe. But I will settle for fortunate coincidence, or just plain dumb luck.

I'm happy either way. As Uncle Dick would have said, "Don't look a chicken in the ass, boy. Just pick up the egg and don't get shit on." Uncle Dick had a way with words. But colorful as I thought he was then, now I prefer a poet's expression: "I rave no more 'gainst time or fate, For lo! my own shall come to me." I can't remember just now who wrote that, but I've quoted it many times. I've studied and taught a lot of poets.

I told Marilyn once that I wish I could believe there really is a heaven where I could go and sit on a cloud or rainbow or something and listen to all the poets all day long. She laughed. And it was a stupid thing for me to say. No matter if there is a paradise as vast as the known universe there is no way a man who has done the things I have done will ever be invited to enter. I have been fortunate to have my poetry here on earth. I know this is not the reason she laughed, though. Marilyn isn't judgmental, and anyway she does not know about all the wrongs I've done.

Our early dates were fun, and by necessity creative. We had no money. An hour sitting on a bench in a secluded area of campus reading the sonnets of Elizabeth Barrett Browning was romantic and met our principal goal of being together. These are beautiful memories to me, although I think they might be a little bit embarrassing to her.

Literature wasn't Marilyn's thing and I took advantage of this in every way I could. She pretended to welcome my help, but now she admits she wanted to get together the same as I did. We were young adults with raging hormones, driven by the urge to mate that is a mark of the human race and every other animal that ever existed. If this weren't so, animal life on this planet surely would have come to an end a few million years ago.

Uncle Dick tried to explain to me about hormones once when I asked about the squirrels playing chasey tail in the middle of winter. He didn't do a very good job, but I understood it had something to do with squirrel sex. He said Mother Nature timed it so the babies would be born in the spring, after it was warmer, and that struck me as a good thing. I told him Mother Nature was very smart.

I do not want this to sound crude. Marilyn and I didn't just latch on to one another for sex. But it is the sex drive that makes males and females attractive to one another and, ultimately, causes us to fall in love. I'm surprised as I look back now that we dated as long as we did before we shared a bed. Her strict upbringing assured she was not going to be rushed into it, and I respected her too much to be unduly demanding. I'm happy for this because, when we did, we coupled more from love than lust and we always will remember it as a beautiful experience.

I know, this is not the language of poets. Poets talk of moonbeams and roses, not hormones. But I defer to Marilyn's view that poets write of the *effects* of love and not the causes. She is the one, given her tendency for analyzing things, who would have been most likely to launch into a discussion of hormones and I probably picked up from her the things I just said.

Without exaggerating, I can tell you that Marilyn would have a good deal more to say when it comes to moonbeams, too. She'd point out that the moon is far more than a mere thing of beauty. Its gravitational pull stabilizes the earth, she says, and controls our tides, keeps the poles from wobbling, and other good things I don't remember because I didn't understand. That's just as well. Like the poets, I prefer to think of the moon merely as a thing of beauty.

I'm tired. I don't feel pain, but I know this is only because of the morphine dribbling through tubes and needles into my bloodstream.

I hear the music again. Led Zeppelin. The frenetic percussion, Jimmie Paige's guitar, Robert Plant vocals. There is a soft spot in my heart for Led Zeppelin because Bucky and I "discovered" them together and because they offered an easy link with students when I first began teaching. The students might not know The Animals or Credence Clearwater Revival, but they all knew Led Zeppelin.

Yes, the music is in my head. Do they play music in hospital rooms? It would be good if they do. I wouldn't know because I have not spent much time in hospital rooms—not ordinary ones like this.

It was different in the war. I had plenty of hospital time then, beginning with a field unit where everybody who came in was an emergency—the intake from all the dustoff calls, shot up and bloody or maimed and broken by artillery shells or rockets or booby traps hidden on jungle trails. Not a lot of time spent on diagnosis. Stop the bleeding, try to spare the leg or arm and keep this one alive a little longer. Not many quick ins and outs.

And getting to a more permanent base didn't change things much in terms of the bottom line. The wards were packed with guys who were barely hanging on and in most cases facing some heavy duty repair work. Bucky and I console each other sometimes that we could have come out of there a lot worse off than we did. Neither of us was left blind or missing limbs or permanently disfigured the way many of those men were.

But then, if we're not careful, this leads to a guilt-trip almost the same as we feel for those who died. These young men weren't killed, but being left maimed so early in life was a terrible price to pay for merely trying to serve their country by doing what they were called on to do. Why did we escape such casualty and they did not?

In some ways my case here isn't all that different from the way it was back there during the war. I didn't come in with a heart attack or cancer or some illness everybody talks about. No routine gall bladder surgery. I'm probably broken now as bad as most of those guys in the Army field hospitals. It's just that I can't tell for sure because I can't hear what people say and I can't feel anything.

I wonder how the doctors and nurses feel about me. Not just me, personally, but cases like me in general. Do they see me as a positive challenge, an incentive to apply their best skills and try to save me? Or am I just in the way, doomed to die soon and meanwhile taking time and space and medicine away from those they might save? Do they know anything about me as a person? Do they know I was in the war? Does it matter to them if they do? I think it would if I were a hero like Uncle Dick, but for those of us from my war I'm not so sure.

What if they know I have killed people? What if they know my passing will make the world a better place? Will they still try to save me? Why should they?

But Marilyn is here. She will tell them I was a teacher. They will see so much good in her they may think there is some good in me. This is as much as I can hope for.

I sense the darkness closing in again, but at the same time I can almost feel the light of Marilyn's presence and this gives me new hope. I want to live to be with Marilyn for years to come. With her at my side I will fight for life as long as a single breath remains. And if they see I am determined to live, maybe the doctors will be more determined to help.

I'm not thinking very well. I may be asking too much of myself. I know my body isn't functioning much at all, and I keep hoping my mind won't fail me. It frustrates me not to be able to think clearly, but more than that it scares me. If my brain stops working it's all over. You probably understand.

12 / *Jan and Phil*

THE EARLY MORNING SUN already was bright in her face as Jan drove into the Memorial Hospital parking lot. She was late for work, which never had happened before. She always had tended toward an exaggerated emphasis on the mechanics of her duty—her work ethic. This was not from a lack of confidence in her training and ability as a nurse, but simply because she saw it as icing on the cake when it came to her record: Jan always does her job, Jan always shows up, Jan always works hard, Jan never is late—until now.

She walked as fast as she could without running from her car to the Wing C entrance and, for once, did not have to wait for an elevator. She was out of breath by the time she arrived at the ICU nurses' station on the sixth floor.

"I'm sorry, guys," she panted. "I didn't hear the alarm this morning. Well, actually I heard it, but went back to sleep before I could drag myself out of bed. Did you do the new shift rounds yet?"

"Well, hell yes," Kendra said, pretending irritation. "We had to get on down the hall and cover for your sorry ass. We've got sick folk here, nurse!"

"Hey, I said I'm sorry."

Kendra dropped the act and grinned. "Everything's up to the minute," she said. "Nurse Marty was more than happy to hold off on the desk work and cover for you."

"Marty—"

"Like she said, I was happy to do it. Since there's no blizzard or anything, we were just hopin' you have an exciting excuse—like a phone call from that good looking man of yours telling you how much he's missed you and can't wait to get home and when he does how he's gonna give you a reason for being late. That's it, right?"

Jan's tension eased with the tolerant reception from her teammates. She liked all the nurses on the floor, but felt lucky to have these two as her most constant companions. They picked her up when she was low and she was confident they would have her back if she ever needed them.

"I only wish," she told Marty. "God, I should have made up something like that just to entertain you with. Emmie has some kind of bug and was up and down all night puking her guts out."

"Poor little thing. Somebody taking care of her?"

"Phil's mother is there. She's real good with the kids. ICU full this morning?"

"Not quite," Marty said, running a finger down a chart on the desk before her. "A couple of discharges overnight. One admitted. Oh, one death."

Jan stiffened. "Oh, no," she said softly. "I hope it was the old fellow in Room 4."

"It was."

"I feel sorry for his wife. She knew he wouldn't make it much longer, but she's going to be pretty much alone now. I don't think there's any other family to speak of."

Kendra pulled a clipboard from a slot below the counter and handed it to Jan. "Here's his story," she said. "You're right. But, hey, the guy was pushing ninety. We do great medicine here, but we can't keep somebody alive forever."

"I know. And he was ready to go. It's just that—"

"It's just that when you're ninety years old you don't have a lot going for you," Marty interrupted. "Remember Methuselah?" She started to sing. "Who calls that livin'—"

Kendra threw up her hands in protest. "Enough! That's disrespectful of the patient."

"Naw, you just don't like my singing," Marty complained. "I didn't mean any disrespect. I was just trying to lighten Jan up a little."

"You guys are too much," Jan said. She was laughing now. "You're both right, as always. That old gentleman had a long and full life, from what I heard. His time had come."

Kendra dropped her defensive posture. "I'll skip the reviews of your singing, Marty. But no more Porgy and Bess! It always breaks me up."

The emotion Jan had felt over news of a patient death quickly vanished. Her shift was back to a normal beginning; she'd be too busy to worry about Emmie.

Minutes later, she began her rounds at Room 12 and found Doctor Arne Morrison already there. He was reading notes on the bedside computer when she walked in, his back to the door, and was startled when she spoke.

"Sorry, Doctor Morrison. I didn't mean to sneak up on you."

"Well, probably just that these old ears don't always hear everything they should hear anymore. Good morning, Jan. How's everything in your world today?"

"Nothing to write home about. How's our guy doing this morning?"

"Nothing new or different from overnight on the computer." He turned and quickly did a cursory hands-on examination of the patient. "Abdominal paracentesis," he said, nodding in her direction. "He's drowning in his own fluids and I don't know exactly where they're all coming from."

"I'll get that set up."

"This one still surprises me. I had him written off from the get-go, as you very well know. But I don't see how he can hang on much longer. If his wife comes in today, could you have me paged, please. I missed her yesterday and I owe her an update I hate to deliver."

"Yes, I'll make sure you get the word."

"Your Guardsman home anytime soon?"

"Two or three days."

"Miss him a lot?"

"Oh, yes! And even more right now, because Emmie's sick."

"Emmie. Your oldest? Nothing serious, I hope!"

"I don't think so. But she was up puking all night."

"Don't let that go on too long. But, hey, you're a real nurse. You know all this stuff without having to hear it from me."

"Always seems kind of different if it's your own, though."

"Well, I know it's hard enough raising kids these days under the best of circumstances. Emmie will be fine. But it would be good to have your husband home, anyway."

The doctor quickly scanned the computer screen. "Get him drained as soon as you can set it up," he said. "Not much else we can do for him now."

"It's at the top of my list."

"I have to tell you, I'm beginning to pull for this guy. By all the standards I know he never should have survived that wreck. He's had enough surgeries to kill a warthog, but he's still hanging on."

"Kill a warthog? I never heard that one before."

"Sure you have. It's a well-known medical term. Probably in all your text books and certainly in all the television doctor shows."

"If you say so, but I'm afraid I missed it."

"Walk down the hall with me, Jan. We can talk some more. Let everybody think it's doctor and nurse stuff. But I want to cuss a little about whoever's threatening to take my favorite nurse's husband away from his family for some half-assed political posturing. I may need you to calm me down."

By the time they reached the nurses' station, the doctor had vented his feelings about the prospect of Phil's Air National Guard unit being deployed. His was not a political agenda; he was concerned about the well-being of guardsmen's families. Jan's spirits were buoyed by his strong support, which she felt was unusual. She had heard very few voices of alarm when it came to possible activation of the Guard.

"Thank you," she told him. "You've made me feel much better about things."

"Don't tell anybody. You wouldn't want to hurt my reputation as a grumpy old man."

Jan turned toward him and, on a sudden impulse, threw her arms around him and hugged him tightly. He waited until she broke the embrace, then squeezed her arm affectionately before walking on down the hall.

"Hey, careful there!" Marty scolded. "I'll bet there is something in the Memorial Hospital code of conduct for nurses about showing proper respect for the institution's god-like physicians and surgeons. Mere nursing personnel shall maintain proper distance at all times and always show their reverence and subservience when in the presence of the great ones."

"Doctor Morrison's not like that."

"Well, maybe not with you, but I could tell you some stories."

"Don't tell me any stories. He's my favorite doctor and I don't want to hear anything negative about him. Where's Kendra?"

"Another bathroom break. She won't admit it, but I think she's experiencing a little early morning sickness."

"Oh, boy! I had forgotten about morning sickness! I thought I'd die when I was pregnant with Emmie."

"God made women so there always would be somebody to suffer, you know. Can you even imagine the complaining we'd hear if the fathers had to go through all the fun things about being pregnant?"

"I don't know. Phil was very supportive."

"Well, I'm afraid he's the exception to the rule. But speaking of Phil, I guess you heard the report on the TV news this morning?"

Jan felt a sudden chill. She knew what Marty was about to tell her. "Oh, no!" she said. "I didn't hear it, but it's not good news. Right?"

"I'm afraid not, honey. I'm sorry. Seems like they are pretty sure now the Air Guard unit is going to be sent to Afghanistan. They sounded like deployment is likely right around the corner."

Jan was stunned by Marty's report. The news was not unexpected, but she had assumed Phil would be home before there was any word on the rumors of his unit's possible orders to the Mideast. He would know before she did, break it to her in a way that was less of a shock, and be there to comfort her the way no one else could.

Emmie's illness, although not serious, had made her more conscious of his absence. The two weeks he'd been away for Guard encampment already seemed like an eternity. How could she manage an absence of a year or more? She felt crushed by the sudden news. She wanted to go somewhere and be alone, away from Marty and Kendra, away from the ICU, away from Memorial Hospital. Surely her emotional state was obvious to anyone who saw her.

She ducked into the nearest restroom and locked the door behind her. The face staring back from the mirror was startling. She was pale—no, beyond pale. She was ghostly white. This face was barely familiar, tired and drawn, matching her feelings, and there was something more. The sparkle in her eyes was missing, replaced by a shadow of fear. And she accepted it now for what it was.

Over the weeks since she had first heard the rumor that Phil's Guard unit might be called to active overseas duty, and especially while he was away in summer camp, her thoughts had centered on how she would miss him if the rumor became fact. She had engaged in self-pity, imagining how she would suffer his absence in silence, how she and the children would miss his love and companionship and wish for his steady hand if a problem should arise, how she would miss his warm body in her bed and lie awake in the middle of the night and yearn for his passionate love-making. But she recognized now that there was a greater concern: Phil would be in war. He could be killed. Disregarding life's usual uncertainties, they had led a sheltered existence and the simple possibility of losing the love of her life had never been a worry. Now, suddenly, it was.

As she stood and stared at her own image in the mirror, Jan's thoughts flashed back over the years. Life's ordinary markers, as she looked back on them now, struck her as monumental turning points. Choices had been made blindly, based on the foreseeable future, but life is filled with causes and effects. One occurrence lead to another, nothing happening by mere chance.

Could it have been that long ago that she first donned her nurse's cap and went to work in a doctor's office in her little home town in Iowa? And how could she have guessed then that this decision would lead her to the man she loved, the father of her children, the man who became more dear to her with every passing day?

An account of their meeting was her personal story, one of only a few she had yet to share with Kendra and Marty. It was a little embarrassing, but they would love it and she would tell them someday. Phil was among the doctor's patients, and the first time she met him was a day he came in with a severe case of tonsillitis and the doctor prescribed a shot of penicillin. Phil gained the honor of being the first patient to whom Jan administered an injection in the buttocks. After fifteen years of marriage, he still joked that it was his nice ass that attracted her.

They made the move to Illinois when he took a job here shortly after the wedding and she worked in the offices of a four-doctor partnership before joining the nursing staff at Memorial Hospital. She had been a part of this sprawling medical institution for fourteen years now and felt as much at home here as she did in their modest house on the west side of town.

And now the stark reality: Without Phil, their house would not be a home. The children would have no father. There would be an unimaginable void in her own life. This fear she had come to embrace would be her new nightmare. As she stood before the mirror and looked squarely into her own eyes, the returning stare was not one of courage. She felt as if she were all alone in the world, desperate for help and knowing there was none.

But she couldn't hide out forever. She had no choice but to go out and face her world. As she had heard Phil lecture the children, "The tougher the situation, the more important it is to tackle it head-on." She splashed cold water on her face and rubbed it briskly with a paper towel until some color returned. She would walk the floor and spend time with patients before she went back to the nurses' station and hope to hide her distress from Marty and Kendra.

Jan didn't recognize the young man coming toward her as she headed for the ICU, but she knew the uniform. His red and black jump suit marked him as a flight nurse on one of the crews of the medevac air ambulance helicopter that came and went from its landing pad atop an adjacent wing of the hospital. He slowed as she came near.

"Are you Jan?" he queried, looking intently at her name tag.

"I'm Jan."

"I'm Greg." He extended a hand. "I'm flight nurse on—"

"I know. I love your uniform. Welcome to the mundane world of us simple floor nurses who don't wear wings."

Greg replied with an appreciative smile. "There are plenty of times when having a floor under my feet all day wouldn't sound too bad. Especially in bad weather. But I wanted flight, and I wouldn't give it up for anything. The reason I was looking for you is, you have a patient we brought in from an accident on Interstate 57 a couple of days ago. A man named—"

"I know who he is. He's right down the hall. Room 12. I'm headed there now."

Greg turned and walked beside her. "I'd like to see him, if you don't mind," he said. "We bring in a lot of people we feel responsible for and then never see them again. Is his wife here, by any chance?"

They had reached the room, and Marilyn was there. Jan introduced Greg, then went about her duties while they talked. There was no change in the patient's vital signs, which she recorded on the bedside computer before speaking briefly with Marilyn and the flight nurse and then moving across the hall to see her next patient.

13 / *I can tell you*

I DON'T KNOW IF THIS really happened or not, but the beautiful place in my dream was familiar. A park with a small lake. Lots of green trees. Marilyn and the kids were there, and we had a picnic basket and a blanket spread on the grass. Craig wanted me to go around the lake with him and I got up and we started to walk. And then, after a few minutes, everything began to change. The lake was a jungle but we walked out of that and then we were in a village. And I knew it was *that* village. And suddenly Craig was running away and screaming and there was shooting all around and I think he was hit but I couldn't find him.

It will never go away. *That* day. *That* place. It was supposed to be a routine search-and-destroy mission. Piece of cake, the captain said. We were relieved to get out of the swamps and jungle and be carried in on Hueys. Before the day was over I cried out for the face of God, but He was nowhere visible. Where was God that day? Was it too much even for Him? Did He have to avert His eyes and turn away? Did God choose to see kindness and beauty elsewhere in His vast universe instead of the horror we saw in that place that day?

I remember a Walt Whitman line that says *real* war never will find its way into books. I'm not sure this is true, but I know what he meant. No matter how vivid my memories, no matter how that day haunts my dreams, my words would not be adequate to make it come alive for you. This may be merciful; that day should be erased from the collective mind of mankind.

War is real only to the warrior. I wake from a deep and troubled sleep and feel again the sheer terror of lying face-down in the mud listening to bullets screaming by in the air over my head or splattering into the ground all around me. I can tell you about it, but you won't feel it. My words could never make it authentic. If you have not experienced war, you never could really understand.

It takes a very good writer to make war seem real. Stephen Crane almost did it in his book, *The Red Badge of Courage*. That's one of my favorites. It's about the Civil War, which came at a terrible cost in lives.

There's never been a good war, but I suppose some have been even more horrific than others. It's hard to see how any could have been worse than mine. Our days were marked by the grinding weariness that overtakes the men in an infantry company rifle squad after constant days and nights of search-and-destroy missions. The enemy we hunted always was elusive and much of the time invisible.

Weeks in combat without a break lead to a sense of hopeless resignation and you know that, sooner or later, your luck is going to run out. There comes a time when you no longer care. It doesn't matter anymore that your only way out may be a body bag. It doesn't matter that you don't know why you're here or what you're fighting for.

At first you pretend it doesn't matter that upon the discovery of a cache of weapons or ammunition hidden in the shack of an old man and woman you will burn their home to the ground—the "destroy" part of the mission—while they stand by and watch without visible emotion. You don't stay to see this because your search never ends.

Pretending does not make this real. You agonize over conflicting spikes of guilt and hard truth that these pitiable villagers may be innocent pawns or they truly may be the enemy. You torch their home without knowing and move on, never looking back, and get ready to do it all over again in the next village you come to. And then, at some point, you no longer have to pretend. It no longer matters.

So you may read about my war and you may see numbers relating to the deaths of human beings and how many years the fighting went on and talk of jungle trails and rice paddies and remote villages and helicopter gunships and napalm and bombing and prisoners and Agent Orange, but you will never know my war as I knew it. And this is just as well; you cannot know my war and ever again feel at peace within yourself.

But I did get out of the war and out of the hospital and out of the Army with one good thing: my new friend, Bucky. When I enrolled at Indiana State University he came to Terre Haute, too, just because I was there. We had decided that going to college was our last best hope of making something positive out of the rest of our lives. We acted more out of desperation than out of any real purpose, I think, but it got us pointed in the right direction.

Bucky was from Kansas City, and had all the street smarts I so sorely lacked. He claimed he never would have survived the tough neighborhood he grew up in had it not been for his two older brothers bailing him out of trouble all the time. I think this was an exaggeration, because the Bucky I know never could have been much of a troublemaker.

Bucky had heard my stories about Uncle Dick and Grandmama and expected Indiana to be a backwoods kind of place, and he was good with that. He said the last place he wanted to be was another big city neighborhood like he grew up in. I think Terre Haute turned out to be pretty much like he thought it would. Anyway, he didn't want to go back to Kansas City after the war and had nowhere else to go.

He wasn't sure what he wanted to study when he got to college. He said he liked working with numbers better than working with people because numbers don't lie, and ended up in accounting. He never questioned my choice to study English, and even encouraged me to focus on poetry if for no better reason than his understanding that poets were gentle people who wouldn't hurt anyone. He said he already had seen enough hurt.

I'd never been there, and Terre Haute would be the biggest town I'd ever lived in. I had no real expectations except that I knew it didn't matter much one way or another. We were out of the war. Some remote corner of Hades would have been an improvement over where we had spent the longest years of our young lives.

It was kind of fun seeing the new college students—kids right out of high school—trying to act grown up and sophisticated. If they hadn't smoked they felt obligated to now, and because they weren't yet of age to go bar-hopping they drank themselves silly at the ubiquitous beer blasts in the fraternity and sorority houses and cramped student apartments. And it wasn't only the new students. While Bucky and I had come of age in the war, most of the young men and women on campus still were cautiously feeling their way into adulthood. We found an almost sadistic pleasure in sitting in dark corners and just watching these newest world citizens make fools of themselves after a few beers.

As you will recognize pretty quickly, though, the joke actually was on us. They got sick and went back to residence halls and dingy apartments and slept it off, while we drank ourselves into stupors hoping that maybe for a few hours alcohol would make the war go away. If it worked, the hours surely were fleeting.

I think you get the picture. We were not model students. It may be that our biggest accomplishment was managing not to get kicked out of school before the end of the first semester. And then Marilyn came along just in time to save us both.

Bucky and Marilyn had a lot in common. She was a city girl from Indianapolis, though hers was a much more genteel neighborhood than Bucky's. And it didn't take us long to figure out that she was a lot smarter than we were.

Marilyn was more interested in the sciences than the humanities, and liked working with anatomy the way Bucky liked working with numbers. She said the physical sciences and the biological sciences have a lot in common. As she put it, "Two plus two always equals four and the toe bone always is connected to the foot bone." She said anything different is an abnormality, and scientists can track it down and probably learn what caused it.

I wish I could tell her, my whole body might be an abnormality right now. I don't think any of my bones are exactly where they ought to be. She would have a clever reply, and she would make me laugh and feel better.

I took a teaching job in Chicago right out of school and Marilyn found a job as a trainer in a fitness center. Bucky came to Chicago, too, and pretty soon was a junior accountant at a small firm that had some big clients. Nita later became a secretary in the office where he worked, and I think it's fair to say he truly was smitten on first sight. I think a lot of the other guys probably were, too.

If you saw Nita, you'd understand. She described herself as "a white girl who got a touch of color and hint of cat eye" from her Indonesian grandmother. She was such a pretty girl I thought of her when I read the words of Oscar Wilde, who referred to a woman as "the willful sunbeam of life."

It was embarrassing sometimes, when we were out with Bucky and Nita at a restaurant or such, how they couldn't keep their hands off one another. They were married after only about three or four months of dating. Turned out she already was pregnant. The baby came early and they lost it. A tiny little girl, who lived only three weeks.

Bucky almost went to pieces. It was his genes that took Nita's baby, he said, and he probably infected it with parasites or something from Vietnam and he would kill himself before it happened again. They had to take him to the white room and if I remember right he was on suicide watch for two or three days. The doctors said Nita shouldn't and maybe couldn't get pregnant again and Bucky felt like he had robbed the world of a beautiful child that would have been a certainty from Nita.

Things are fading in and out. I think I'm still awake, but I can't be sure.

I know I was talking about Bucky and Nita and the baby, but this might have been a dream. I think my brain gets tired of unhappy memories and tries to fool me into believing something better. If what I told you ended well it was a dream, because the real story did not have a happy ending. If I told you they lost the baby I am awake and remembering real things and not dreams.

So this is what happened. Annie was born not long afterwards. I could tell how much it hurt Bucky to see her, a healthy baby girl, and I felt guilty that our child survived and his didn't. It didn't seem fair, and Bucky's and Nita's loss took a lot away from the joy Marilyn and I found in our own firstborn. Over the years, I tried a few times to talk to Bucky about the baby. He just refused to discuss it, and I finally picked up on the fact that anything that reminded him was likely to lead to a night of heavy drinking and I was careful never to bring it up again. I can only hope and trust that the passing years have helped erase his pain.

It was hard to tell how Nita felt. She only showed a kind of calm detachment, like it happened to someone else instead of her. Marilyn said Nita was immensely affected by the loss, like a part of her own body had been stolen away and she knew it never would be returned. She thought Nita recognized her own beauty and, like Bucky, felt she ought to be able to produce a beautiful child. It was even tougher because the baby was a girl, Marilyn said.

I feel like there's something crawling on my face. It's a pretty indefinite sensation, like a feather swinging over my head and only touching skin here and there. This may be progress, though, because I don't think I could have felt this before. But it's hard to make much out of it as long as I can't touch myself anywhere and find out if I'm actually getting some feeling back.

If there really is something crawling on my nose, Marilyn will notice. She'll brush it off and that will be the end of it. If Annie sees it, she'll pluck it up and see what it is and consider how to keep it alive and give it a new chance somewhere else. Annie doesn't want to kill anything.

But there may be nothing there. I don't know if I could tell, and I can only feel my skin from the inside out. I read once that nerve endings don't remember pain, otherwise the accumulation of a lifetime of even little hurts would overwhelm us. But could I smell smells and taste tastes or hear sounds embedded by sensory perceptions from the past? Could there be a tiny cluster of brain cells somewhere beneath my skull struggling to dredge these up and fling them out to prove I'm still alive?

This is all new territory for me. I have no training in physiology or anatomy or cell structure or brain function or anything else that might help me understand what's going on. I work with words, and my body is not made up of words. I have no control over my body now. I wish I could scream for help but there is nothing I can do, like I'm no longer an animate object.

Is this where the music comes in? I think I hear the music when my brain gets tired and these little clusters of cells do their best to make themselves known. I hear it now. Fleetwood Mac. The music with wild abandon, on the beat driven by Mick Fleetwood himself, the percussion master always in full control. I will let the music rule. I will be Lindsey Buckingham and get down on my knees and be touched by adoring fans even as I assault the strings of my guitar, then dance across the floor to embrace Stevie Nicks and she will look at me with those big, brown Stevie Nicks eyes.

Nita's eyes, dangerous, lonely, hungry. I'm being pulled in again. I don't want to be. I won't be. That's how it happened before. I'm sorry, Marilyn. I'm sorry, Bucky. I'm sorry.

Make the music go away.

14 / Marilyn and Greg

MARILYN STRUGGLED to keep her emotions in check as she greeted Greg. Her husband had told her once that for Vietnam veterans suffering from post-traumatic stress disorder, the sound of a helicopter would be one of the most frequent triggers of anxiety episodes. He steadfastly denied suffering PTSD himself, but said if he did have it "hearing a chopper" wouldn't bring problems because, for him, the sound brought back good memories of his medevac rescue.

She doubted he even was aware he'd had a second life-saving air ambulance transport, but she had hoped for an opportunity to express her gratitude to the flight crew for their role in saving his life just as he'd always wished the same after his rescue in the war. This was one of the few things he ever had talked about when it came to his time in Vietnam.

"I'm grateful for what you did," she said to Greg. "I know he owes his life to you and your team. He wouldn't have made it without you."

Greg shook his head. "He already had had life-saving attention when we got him," he said. "But, yes, we knew we needed to get him here as quick as possible. The pilot ran at full throttle, straight in. That's what we do best."

"You gave him a chance, even though it looks pretty thin."

Greg put a hand on her shoulder. "I'm sorry. I was hoping things looked better."

"He used to talk about the sound of a Huey helicopter like it was a band of angels singing, or something. He always says he owes his life to a medevac team and I know he would feel the same way again now."

"We knew he was in Vietnam, because he kept saying 'dustoff' on the way in. You may know, that was the radio code for a medevac rescue call over there. And, yeah, they flew the Bell HU-1 Iroquois, the Huey, for medevac and everything else."

"He doesn't like to talk about the war, but I know he thinks he would have died if they hadn't got him to a field hospital pretty quick. He almost certainly would have lost an arm."

Greg nodded. "And those guys usually went in under fire. One of our trainers was flight nurse on a medevac crew in Vietnam and he said they felt like clay pigeons almost every time they landed. We have some pretty touchy places to land sometimes, but nobody is shooting at us."

"Do you get a lot of accidents?"

"Oh, yeah. Way too many. Thank God most of them are not as bad as the one he was in. I assume you know there were a couple of fatals in it?"

"That's what I heard. I heard they were elderly."

"They were. An older couple from St. Louis. I guess they were in a van with several people in it and one of their grandchildren was hurt, too, but that's all I know. I wanted to tell you, though, because it's something a lot of people ask, he didn't suffer a lot of pain. The guys who did all the first aid before we got him said he had a pretty good head bump and had been unconscious ever since they pulled him out. And of course we gave him plenty of pain killer on the way in."

"Thank you for that," Marilyn told him. "The doctor tells me he doesn't feel anything now. That's all I can ask."

Greg stepped closer to the bed in the middle of the room and looked down at the patient. "I'm sorry for what you're going through," he said. "All we can do is hope for the best. But I just wanted to check up on him. I'm glad I got to meet you. And by the way, I almost forgot, just like in the movies he said your name a couple of times while we were getting him all strapped in. I should have told you that."

Marilyn burst out laughing. "I'm sorry," she said, "That just struck me as funny. You see it in a movie or read it in a book and it sounds hokey. But you hear it in real life, it's a whole different thing. Thank you for telling me that, even if you just made it up."

Greg laughed, too. "Yeah, I get it. But it really happened. Look, I've got to get moving. I'm sorry I had to meet you under these circumstances, but I'm glad you were here. Good luck." He paused as he was about to leave the room, and turned back. "I'm grateful to him for serving his country," he said. "A man with his record deserves better than this. I'm sorry."

He was only a few steps down the hall when Marilyn heard his phone ring. At the same instant, the engine started on the medevac helicopter sitting on its pad, ready for launch. She watched as he rushed to the elevators, grateful for his visit.

Back beside her husband's bed, she looked down and smiled. "You said my name," she said softly. "Thank you, sweet man. I don't know if you even are aware I'm here, but I'm not going to leave you. We've put in way too much time together to break the chain now."

She thought back on the things Greg had told her. There was something she needed to do. She went looking for Jan, and met her head-on as Jan came out of a room a few doors away.

"Could I ask you something?" Marilyn asked.

"Of course. What is it?"

"The flight nurse said there were children injured in the wreck. Do you know if any of them happen to be here in the hospital and if it would be okay for me to visit them if they are?"

Jan took a second to try and remember what she might have heard. "I don't know, honey," she said then, "but I'll see if I can find out. If you've got a minute, come along with me."

They went to the nurses' station and Jan got on the phone. It didn't take her long to find the answer to Marilyn's question. Four children had been hurt in the accident, two of them seriously. Both of the latter were in Memorial Hospital, on the floor above.

"The family of one of the kids asked that no visitors be permitted," she told Marilyn. "That's the girl. You would be welcome to visit the boy."

Marilyn said she would visit the child later in the day, and thanked Jan for checking this out. "And I know how things work around here," she kidded. "Sooner or later I will be asked to evaluate everybody who so much as smiled at me and I will make sure to give you a five-star review."

Marty had been waiting alongside Jan for the information to come in, quietly reserved. "Dang, girl, that's some good detective work," she said. "I wasn't sure you could get that information without knowing an actual name to begin with. Hey, as they say in Hollywood, 'good on ya!'"

"How do you know what they say in Hollywood?"

"Hey, Matthew McConaughey writes me and calls all the time. I talk Hollywood as good as anybody."

Jan wagged a finger. "Your mama taught you better than to tell whoppers like that." And then to Marilyn, "Just be sure it's Janice you award the gold stars to and not Janet, as Doctor Morrison usually calls me. Do you need help finding that room?"

Marilyn assured her she would have no problem. She wasn't sure why, but she felt better just knowing she might connect with other families affected by the accident. She needed to go back to Room 12 first, though, because Bucky was coming.

He was there when she got to the room.

"You're a sweetheart, Bucky," she greeted him. "The sight of you lifts my spirits faster than anything else I can think of."

He offered a wide smile. "Maybe I should have been in the movies or something," he joked. "I hear that people pay admission for that. Getting their spirits lifted, I mean. You doing okay?"

"Yeah, I heard some good things from the medevac flight nurse that brought him in from the wreck. I was about to go upstairs and see a little boy who was hurt in the accident. Want to come with me?"

"I suppose I could. What do you know about him?"

"Nothing, really. It's just that, I don't know, it feels like there is a common bond or something. I thought his parents might feel as alone as I have and it might give them a lift just having someone else going through the same thing to sympathize with. I guess that's kind of silly."

"No, it's not. It's very considerate. I'll go with you."

When they got to the child's room, they found a privacy curtain drawn around the patient's bed and a young girl sitting in a chair in a corner playing a game on her phone. The girl looked up and smiled.

"Mama just went to the bathroom," she said. "Are y'all here to see Zeke?"

"Yes, I think so," Marilyn told her. "What's your name?"

"Georgette."

"That's a pretty name you don't hear very often. Is Zeke your brother?"

"Yes. I was named after my daddy."

Bucky was about to comment on this when Zeke's mother arrived. Her surprise on finding the visitors in the room was obvious. "I'm sorry," she said. "I didn't expect to find—"

Marilyn interrupted. "We're the ones who should be sorry. We don't want to intrude, but we understand that the child who is a patient here was in an accident on the interstate. My husband was in it, too, and was seriously injured."

"Oh, I'm sorry to hear that. Zeke got a broken leg and some fractured ribs, but he's doing very well and I think his doctor is going to let him come home to-morrow. They just wheeled him off to radiology. The young man who took him said it would probably take about twenty minutes."

Bucky motioned toward Georgette, who was stand-ing now. "This pretty little girl belong to you, too?"

"She does. Most of the time, anyway. If you'd been here an hour ago I might have been ready to give her away. But we all get a little cranky when we're tired."

Georgette giggled, and pushed tighter against her mother's side.

"Look," Marilyn said, "we don't want to invade your privacy. We just wanted to check on your son, and hope he is doing well. I guess it was just a feeling of all being in this together. You know what I mean?"

"Oh, sure I do. There were a lot of people whose lives got turned upside down in that big wreck. You don't think about things happening like that until they do. Do you folks live around here?"

"I live in Chicago," Bucky said. "Marilyn and her husband live in southern Illinois. He was on his way to Chicago to visit me when he got in the accident. Where do you live?"

"Nashville. We were on our way to Wisconsin for a few days of cool vacation. I guess we made it about half way."

Marilyn shook her head. "I'm so sorry. Was Zeke the only one hurt?"

"My husband was banged up a little, but nothing serious. Zeke was in the front passenger seat and not wearing his seat belt. His father had just got on him about it. I guess next time he'll listen. "

"Is your husband here?"

"He went on up to Wisconsin this morning. That's where his family is and he needed to get things together—insurance, a new car, all that. He will be back tomorrow to pick us all up."

"I get to see my cousins," Georgette said, her face brightened by her excitement.

Bucky reached over and offered her a high-five. "Cousins are good to have," he said. "I'll bet you don't get to see them much if they live in Wisconsin and you live in Tennessee."

Georgette slapped his hand. "Only just at times like now," she said. "They hardly ever come down to visit us in Nashville."

Marilyn was about to say something to Georgette when there was a sudden swirl of activity. The patient was being returned to his room, clearly enjoying his place as the center of attention. He gave a thumbs-up to his mother and chided the attendants pushing his bed for being "crooked drivers," but thanked them for delivering him safely and offered a mock salute.

"I hope he didn't give you a hard time like he does me," his mother said to one of the young men bringing him in.

The attendant seemed ready to play along with the patient, giving him a big frown. But then he turned back to Zeke's mother, with a smile. "Not at all," he said. "He's a brave young man. He told us he has to be able to handle injuries because he's going to be a soldier, like his daddy was."

Zeke's mother turned to Marilyn. "His father was in the Army and served in Iraq," she said. "Zeke just loves seeing him in his uniform. He says he can't wait until he's old enough to join."

15 / *I remember his words*

I KNOW THE ACCIDENT just happened, but the war still seems like it was only yesterday, too, and I don't even know anymore how long it's been. Marilyn might know, but we've never talked much about the war. That's my fault. She used to ask me about it and she could understand I didn't want to tell her. She says I don't have to talk about it if I don't want to and she won't ask me anymore.

I've never talked much about it with anyone but Bucky, except for answering questions from an Army investigator and a few sessions with a counselor when I was in college. That captain kept asking me questions I didn't want to answer, but the counselor helped me feel better about a couple of things.

During the war I thought Uncle Dick would understand. But when I got home he acted like he knew things I'd never told him, and I think some of what he believed was wrong. I had heard plenty about his war, but he never wanted to hear about mine. He said things one day that hurt me very much, especially coming from him, and I still remember his words. He said we disgraced the uniform. Things were never the same after that. I saw him occasionally but he seemed different and we didn't talk much anymore. After I started school and Marilyn came along I hardly saw him at all. My biggest regret is that he never got to really know Marilyn.

In good conscience, I can't blame Uncle Dick too much. Everyone knew I wasn't a hero.

I think Marilyn's still here. I was hoping Annie would show up. I'm afraid Craig won't come. He's off in the wilds of Alaska looking for gold and I doubt they even tried to reach him. He'll check in with his mother sooner or later, but she very well may tell him not to bother coming because there is nothing he can do and I probably wouldn't know he was here.

This may already have happened. But I hope not, because I dearly want to see him. I have things I should talk to him about.

Craig marches to his own drummer. I used to worry about him all the time, but not anymore. He has a solid head on his shoulders and knows what he wants from life. I envy him the freedom to do the things he wants to do, while he can. Life is short. And I'm eternally grateful he did not have to go to war. I never thought about the terror of having a son or daughter in war until I became a parent, myself. After being in war, I don't think I could take it.

Annie and Craig were always good kids, and they turned out to be good adults. Annie's Bryan is the best son-in-law we could have asked for and we love Jody, even though she and Craig didn't last long as a couple. Annie made me a grandfather when I felt like I was too young, but once I held that baby in my arms age didn't matter. That beautiful little boy was my own flesh and blood and my heart filled with love that was fresh and new. And different. Easier, less stressful. This time no responsibility came with it. I had never felt this before— the absolute joy of love with no strings attached—and I reveled in it then and I still do.

There have not been many great events in my life, especially if you count tragedy separately. The day I married Marilyn is one and the births of Annie and Craig are at the top of the list, too. But when you become a father, you know you have a new level of accountability, babies to care for and protect as well as to love and cherish.

If things are as they should be, grandchildren don't come with the extra duty. Between them, Annie and Craig made me a grandfather five times over. I love them all, but none of the other four was quite the same as the first.

Annie's been a good mother to her three. Craig's marriage ended too soon for him to have much of a chance and I don't think he wanted children to begin with. He wasn't ready. Since his breakup with Jody we've hardly seen those two little grandsons at all. I doubt they'll know me the next time they see me, if I make it out of here. I would like to be a part of their lives and I hope I get that chance. They need their father, too, and I probably should talk to Craig about this. I *will* talk to Craig about it. I can speak from experience. This is another obligation I need to live for.

I got an extended family when I married Marilyn, of course. Her parents welcomed me, but it took a while to gain the trust of her sister, Margie. Margie is five years older and watched over Marilyn like a mother hen. I like Margie very much and wish my sisters had even once shown the same concern for me that she's always shown for Marilyn.

The first time I met Marilyn's father I started to address him as "Mister" and he demanded that I call him Mack. He hated formality. Mack was an unskilled laborer who worked in building construction and never managed to make much of a living, but he may have been the most honest man I've ever known. He thought raising a family was the most important work a man can do, and I've no doubt he actually went hungry some days so the girls could have more. He wore his pride in his two daughters like a badge of honor.

I think I hurt over Mack's death even more than Marilyn did. Her mother, Betty, died less than a year later, and Marilyn said her mother just lost the will to live after she lost her husband. I guess this is how it is when a good man dies.

It was clear that Mack trusted me to give Marilyn a better life. I'm not sure why, except that he didn't know what I did in the war. I want to honor his memory by leaving his daughter a lasting gift of true love. Not that this has been lacking, but I have not expressed my feelings the way I should have.

I want to make love to Marilyn again. I want to tell her she still is my soul-mate, the center of my universe. I want to tell her sharing my bed with her never ceased to be a thrill, that waking in the middle of the night and arousing her or being aroused by her and making love and melding two bodies as one made my life good. I want to tell her that lying awake and merely touching her body brought comfort on countless difficult nights when the war would not go away. And I want to tell her that finding her and having her agree to be my wife was the thing that mattered above all else in my life, that having her as the mother of my children makes me the most fortunate of all men.

Being able to say these things to Marilyn is what I want most, but there are other things that matter. I want a chance to smooth things over after my falling out with Annie. The good thing is, this won't involve hard stuff like struggling to find common ground. Annie and I understand and love and respect each other and love being together. What has been missing is my apology, my assurance that I know I should have been more thoughtful and that I hope she will let me try to get it right.

I'm scared. I sense the darkness closing in again. It is not the darkness I fear, but the inherent danger that once it comes I might never see light again. I can't undo the things I've done and I don't deserve another chance, but I desperately want one—not another lifetime, nor even a few golden years, but time enough to repay at least some small part of the immense debt I owe to people I love.

I remember a Shelley poem that says gleams of a more remote world visit the soul in sleep. This would be that vision of heaven I talked about. I've always liked Shelley's poetry. He wrote a lot about death and dying, but it was like he saw these in a brighter light than most poets.

It would be comforting to believe there was a heaven you'd go to after you died. I remember how Chaplain Lewis used to rave about the Kingdom of Heaven like he thought it was a real place. I don't know if he did, but he made you feel good just by the way he talked. He was a husky infantry captain who played football at the University of Tennessee and everyone liked him and you didn't completely believe everything he said but you wanted to think he wouldn't say it if it wasn't true.

I wish I could sort things out better before I go under again, but there are too many images rushing in and out. Sounds and smells, too, but I can't tell which ones are real and happening now and which ones have been just lying there waiting to pop out. They all run together—the screech of rubber tires on concrete and gunfire in the distance and crunching metal and flashing lights and helicopters landing and sirens and people yelling and the smell of something burning. And I see bleeding bodies.

Don't think it selfish of me, but I wish Chaplain Lewis was here now. Even if I didn't know it, I wish he was standing over me saying a prayer or simply talking about the Kingdom of Heaven the way he did. And then I wish Marilyn and Annie and Craig were here, too, and could hear his beautiful words. And then, if I die, they will feel better.

16 / *Jan and Marilyn*

J an ALWAYS FELT A STRONG personal connection with patients in her charge, even those who were short-term and "just numbers" as Kendra would say. They were living men and women and children and she deemed it an almost sacred obligation to give them the best care she could. When they were discharged, she hoped it was because they were well and had no further need for her service. If patients died, she hoped their passing was expected and their families would be able to say they had the best of treatment and spent their final hours on earth without suffering. But she viewed life as precious; it should not be surrendered easily.

She had developed a keen sense of *esprit de corps* with the other nurses on the floor and believed they all were as committed to their profession as she was. This wasn't something she had felt in the beginning, but the result of years watching them work. Should Phil or one of the children be sick enough to require hospitalization, God forbid, she would be content to have them in the care of any one of her fellow nurses here at Memorial Hospital.

Marty liked to assert her independence by proclaiming that nurses do not wear uniforms anymore, but Jan occasionally found herself almost wishing that they did. Uniforms meant service. She recognized the critical role of police and firefighters and various emergency medical technicians in the roles of first responders. Both her father and an uncle had served in the U. S. Army. She was proud of Phil for serving in the Air National Guard, too, even though his service was beginning to come at a price on the family.

When she brought up the subject of nurses' uniforms with Phil one day, he joked that it was a simple mark of conceit; she knew she would look good in a uniform. This was true, to a point. Phil regularly encouraged this view by teasing that he married her for her overall sexy beauty, "not just your tits," and thought she'd look sensational in a uniform of any kind. But she was confident it was the uniform itself that appealed to her and not the image of her in it. Being of service to those who needed her was much more important than her appearance.

It had been a long day and Jan was tired, but before she left the hospital she wanted to spend a few minutes in Room 12. She worried about this patient more than any of the others, perhaps going beyond what was appropriate by nursing standards. She had been trained to maintain an objective relationship and be careful not to let an emotional bond develop.

But this man defied the odds against survival primarily through his own tenacious will to live. This was not just her own view, but also what she had been told by Doctor Arne Morrison. Doctor Morrison's years of experience certainly qualified him as an authority and Jan placed enormous trust in his word.

How near to death had this patient been when he was wounded in the war in Vietnam decades earlier? Had he been forced to fight for life then as he was now? How much had his own determination contributed to his survival? He was in a struggle now she felt he was destined to lose in the end, but it was clear he was holding on to the last breath.

Jan's deep regard for this patient as an individual was only one factor in her mounting sense of personal connection, though. Another, perhaps equally strong, was her concern for Marilyn. She had worried from the outset that Marilyn's was a solitary vigil, and was grateful when Bucky showed up to be at her side. If there were sisters, children, and grandchildren, surely it was time for some of them to appear.

When she got to Room 12, she found Marilyn there, standing beside her husband's bed. The room was deathly quiet.

"I see you're standing watch all by yourself again," Jan said.

"Sure. But it's kind of what I do."

"I thought your friend was going to be here for a while. Is he gone?"

"Bucky? He had to go back to Chicago and catch up on a couple of things at work. I hope he gets back tonight, but I don't know if he'll make it. He will be here tomorrow, though."

"I hope so. I'm glad he's here for you."

Marilyn moved to the chair by the wall. "Bucky's my anchor," she said. "I don't know if I could have made it through this without him."

"Everybody needs all the support they can get at times like this. He and your husband seem to be very close."

"They were in the war together. Vietnam, I mean. I think they feel like it's them against the world. At one time I resented being kept out to some extent, but a counselor explained that their bond is based on a common background I could never share and helped me to understand why they lean on each other the way they do."

Jan took a place in the chair beside her. "He's lucky to have a wife who understands. You have, what, two children? Are they as understanding as you are?"

Marilyn seemed unsure how to answer. "You know, I think they are," she said. "Their relationship is different, of course. And they were not here in the early years, when he used to have complete emotional breakdowns sometimes. Terrible nightmares, and all that."

"Are they coming?"

"I think our daughter will be here tomorrow, and my sister is on her way from Philadelphia. I'm not sure about our son. He's way up in Alaska somewhere prospecting for gold."

Jan laughed. "Seriously? I didn't know anybody did that anymore."

"They do. Craig's certain he's going to strike it rich one of these days. I know he'll get here as soon as he can, but who knows how long it may take. He was probably a hundred miles from civilization when he got the word."

"Well, we have to be thankful for all the modern technology that connects us, I guess. I don't know about you, but I have a serious love/hate relationship with my cell phone. You know, I can't live with it—"

"And can't live without it. Oh, yes. I feel the same way."

Jan stood, and put a hand on Marilyn's shoulder. "I'm going to have to get along," she said. "I've got a sick daughter at home. But I'll be back bright and early in the morning and I'll be okay with it if I don't find you here. You need to get some sleep, okay?"

"I hear you. Don't worry. I'm going to the motel in an hour or so and once I hit the mattress I may not wake up for a week. I hope your daughter is doing better."

As Jan walked to the elevators, she felt a surge of melancholy. Even if Marilyn's children got here in time, they simply were coming to preside over their father's death. She sensed that Marilyn was prepared for this, having stood beside his bed and witnessed the almost complete absence of life already. Would the son and daughter be equally ready for what lay in store? Their entire lifetime of experience with their father had lacked anything comparable to what they faced now. Marilyn, on the other hand, had been through the early years after Vietnam, when he would have been in his most fragile emotional state. Surely she had come to appreciate the tenacity with which he fought his battles, but recognized now that he was in a fight he could not win.

Her heart ached for this wife and mother, a complete stranger until a few days ago. *War does such awful things to people.* And then she thought about Phil, and the likelihood he was going to be called to active duty in a far away, dangerous part of the world. She was counting the hours until he got home, but how long would he be here? Being married to a man in the Air National Guard was not the same as being married to one in the regular armed forces and the whole topic of possible active duty deployment was one she'd never expected to deal with. But now she had to.

Marilyn would not be the only one finding it hard to sleep tonight.

17 / *I remember my father*

I HOPE WHATEVER THEY ARE doing to me will help make breathing easier. The difference is subtle, but it seems like I have to work harder to get air. I doubt they know this, though, and don't really expect them to do anything about it. But they are doing something to me, or around me. Around my body. This is no longer me.

I know the odds are against me, and if my continued existence is not in the cards I will try to face death with more courage than I've had in life. I never had the courage to fight for the right things and I didn't care if I died. But I'm paying a price for this now, with death staring me in the face. I'm still ready to die but not until I have one last chance to make amends. I have lain here these hours since the accident counting the reasons I have for wanting another chance.

Because I'm a teacher, people may expect me to have advice on how to raise children, but I don't. I've done a poor job with my own. I'm conflicted over too many things to believe I might have anything to offer other parents. I'll defer to Kahlil Gibran, who said giving of ourselves is what matters, not giving of possessions. I may be rationalizing some on this because Marilyn and I never really had much in the way of possessions to offer. She certainly has given freely of herself, though, and I have tried to follow her example. But I know deep down there were many times I didn't try hard enough.

Marilyn would say I'm taking refuge behind the words of others again, that I do this too often. She says this is a lazy way to avoid having to come up with words of my own and making a real commitment. I'm grateful she didn't know the Rudyard Kipling lines, "He wrapped himself in quotations—as a beggar would enfold himself in the purple of emperors." I have not told her I disagree, but I don't think it is being lazy so much as it is recognizing my own limitations.

Poets talk of moonbeams and I talk of mud and sand because I've wallowed plenty in mud and sand and I've never spent much time in moonbeams. It's easier to try to explain something when you actually have been there.

Sorry, my mental processes are getting all twisted again. Without my normal senses, nothing seems right. I cannot hear the sounds and see the images that actually surround me now, but I hear sounds and see images in my mind. If memory is made up of perceptions stored in the brain it's like my storage space is filled and things are spilling out haphazardly without waiting to be called up.

Maybe this argues against my own reasoning, about experience. Your experience is only as good as the memory stored in your brain.

But if I remember the words of Kahlil Gibran surely my memories of war and people and things that happened in my life are accurate, if only I can call them to the surface in some logical order. If I can concentrate on parenting or teaching or Bucky's funny walk or whatever, I might gain more control over the flow of what runs through my mind.

To the point of parenting, then, I think the reason I've never been confident I was a good father is because I never had that relationship in my own childhood. I was pretty much raised by my grandmother and Uncle Dick. My mother worked full time at a small shop where most of the women in town bought their clothes and then waitressed at an all-night diner, probably seven days a week.

I think I was only about four years old when my father left. But I remember lying in bed at night when he came home, hoping he would check on me the way he did my sisters. He never did. I don't think he ever said he loved me. I tried to be good so he would like me, too, but I guess he just favored girls.

I used to wonder, during the war, whether my father even would know if I got killed. I knew he wouldn't care. I found out this wasn't too unusual, and a lot of the guys in Vietnam didn't have fathers at home. But I'd guess most of them probably knew their fathers and had spent time with them at some point in their lives.

It still bothers me that my father left before I was old enough to know him. My sisters remember him, and seem to have loved him. I think he was a coward who ran out on our mother and left her with nothing. I always wanted to confront him someday and see if he could look me in the eye and make excuses for what he did. My mother deserved better.

Marilyn told me one time I should thank my father for my love of poetry, and in her style, "It's the onliest thing he ever did for you." She knows how my grandmother read to me from a little book of Tennyson poems from as early as I can remember and how I would sit on Grandmama's lap and her voice was gentle and loving and maybe the closeness had something to do with it, but I loved the language of poems. She knows I wanted to talk like that, even when I was a little kid, and she understands why.

And Marilyn is happy for me, that I have the poetry to love and that I wanted to teach it to the students, and she tells me she knows I was a good teacher and my students were fortunate and maybe some of them came to love the poetry, too, and I can take credit for this. I'm not sure all this is true—I doubt it, in fact—but I love her for saying these things. It's not her nature to exaggerate and she is doing it just for me.

Bucky doesn't understand my love of poetry the way Marilyn does. He doesn't see beauty in words. He would never read a poem. But he likes science fiction, and reads more than he pretends. Bucky likes numbers. I guess it's like Uncle Dick always said, "There's lots of different trees in the forest and lots of different fishes in the sea." But I remember one day when Bucky was feeling sorry for himself and thought I looked down on him because he didn't know poetry and Marilyn told him he'd have reason to exist long after I did because I could exhaust every word of every language ever spoken and he would still be counting all the stars in the universe.

Because it was Marilyn who told him, he felt better and said everything was okay. I sometimes think if Marilyn told Bucky he could fly he'd try jumping off a tall building just to see.

When I got older I used to get Grandmama's little book of Tennyson from time to time and just sit in a quiet place and read the poems and feel like I was safe from the world. Tennyson was my escape. My favorite reading place was in the woods. I could walk along a creek that ran through Uncle Dick's farm and find a place to sit and enjoy the solitude I wanted.

Even if I didn't have the book, I might sit for hours and relish the feeling of being in a remote, private world separated from anything that made me unhappy. I felt connected to the squirrels that played in the big oak and hickory trees and skittered around on the ground hunting nuts and acorns and gathering dried leaves to build nests once it began to turn cold in the fall. And there was a den of foxes on the creek. When new litters came along, the baby foxes would come right up to me and try to figure out who I was and never seem to worry I might be a dangerous intruder.

Uncle Dick was very much an outdoorsman, but I never knew if it was because he wanted to be outside or just needed to get out of the house. Grandmama always said Aunt Nell made his life hard. The two of them—Grandmama and Aunt Nell—never got along very well. I didn't like to go in Aunt Nell's house because she always worried that I was going to get something dirty or break something, and anyway I'd rather be outside with Uncle Dick.

It probably was dangerous, but he would let me ride with him on his old John Deere tractor while he plowed his fields and worked up the soil making it ready for planting corn or wheat and, later, cultivating and other things he didn't explain to me. When he was on the tractor and I didn't want to ride or it was too dusty or he said I couldn't for some reason, I often played in his big barn.

I did like Aunt Nell's garden, though. She had lots of flowers and there was a little statue on each of the four corners of the garden plot—three angels and the Christ child. She was very proud of these. She claimed they were alabaster, but Uncle Dick said they were molded and glazed concrete. I think her garden was the only place I ever saw delphinium. I thought it was beautiful. It was a long time before I learned what it was, but it turned out to be one of those things that, once you learn, you never forget.

As much as I liked his company, I did not always agree with Uncle Dick. He used to talk about fox hunting like it was grand sport and he envied those who were able to play. I couldn't understand how anybody could hunt animals and I thought if they ever saw them as babies they never would hunt them again. He said he didn't think they actually killed the foxes, but I asked why they hunted them then and he got irritated and wouldn't talk about it anymore and said anyway he'd rather hunt squirrels. I didn't like that, either.

I could no more imagine seeing anyone kill squirrels or baby foxes in the woods along the Ohio River than I could imagine seeing anyone kill children in the war. Now I know better. I wish I didn't.

I came to love solitude, but Marilyn says all that time in the woods just made me a loner. She grew up in the city, and doesn't understand how different it was for me living in a little town and spending much of my time in the country with few other kids around. During the summer, when school was out, mine was very much an adult world in which I was left to entertain myself.

Uncle Dick always wished I could play baseball. He said every boy should. But he understood that there were not enough boys around to get up a game.

I took my radio into the woods, too, and spent hours listening to the most popular rock music station in Louisville. The Beetles and The Rolling Stones entertained me, and I liked The Byrds without knowing they didn't spell their name with an "i." I was certain I was destined to be a guitar player in a rock band. Never mind that I had no guitar and couldn't have played it if I did.

My grandmother gave me her little book of Tennyson poetry when I was about to leave home and I carried it with me in Vietnam. It helped me then, too, though when I needed it most there wasn't much time to read. It probably is a miracle it didn't get lost. Sad to say, I don't know where it is now. I wish I had it.

When we're young and innocent and protected from the real world we think we have a whole lifetime ahead to follow whatever path happens to open before us. It never occurred to me then that I might be a teacher. But after the war, when I had a chance to go to college and had to think about what I wanted to do, it struck me that I could spend the rest of my life immersed in the works of Tennyson and other giants of poetry and literature. Their words had offered me shelter and brought me comfort when I needed it most and I wanted to share this and thought it was one contribution I could make to creating a better world.

Don't get me wrong. Nobody could be more aware than I that I'm an imperfect messenger, but being a teacher and doing the best I could to add something of value to the lives of those boys and girls was good to do. I am ashamed of many things I've done, but I am grateful I had those years in the classroom and I hope I helped some of the kids I taught find shelter and comfort, too. I hope Marilyn is being honest when she says the good things she says, and even though she exaggerates I believe she is.

I wish my grandmother was here now. I wish I could hear her gentle voice instead of the sounds of highway crashes and fire fights and family quarrels and wounded men and dying mothers and babies and wanton acts of personal gratification that for a given instant seemed right even though I knew they were wrong. But once written, our life story can never be erased. What I did hurt other people and you ought not to be allowed just to walk away from that like you never did anything you knew wasn't right.

My grandmother passed away many years ago, of course, and my mother is gone, too. It's funny how we don't want to say "died" when we are talking about someone we love. It's like death is forever and nobody's ever ready for it and passing away is somehow less permanent. When I was a little boy I wondered why old people didn't worry more about dying. I asked Grandmama about this but she didn't want to talk about it because she said it made her sad.

Uncle Dick showed me an old burial site on a bluff overlooking the Ohio River where there was only one grave stone. The inscription on it was the first poem I ever learned: "Remember friend, as you pass by, as you are now, so once was I. As I am now, so you must be. Prepare for death and follow me."

I didn't know the technicalities of first person voice and all that, of course, but I asked Uncle Dick how they could pretend this was written by somebody who already was dead and buried and if they didn't pretend this how come it said "I"? Why didn't it say "Grandpa" or whoever was buried there? Uncle Dick complained that I asked too many questions and said next time he wasn't going to show me something interesting.

We go through much of life taking for granted the strong bonds of family, whether blood or marriage. It's as if we assume they will be there forever. The bonds inevitably are broken as we grow old, because the older generation passes on even as the younger generation arrives. I had started to feel this in the last couple of years in ways I never felt it before, and if I had a second chance I would relish those bonds and cling to family with all the power of my body and spirit.

I may not have a second chance, though. I may have only a little time left. If I die tomorrow will my loss be mourned by many? Or will my passing be marked by little more than the hole left in the glass of water when I pull out my thumb, like my father said? I could make a game of wondering who really will miss me when I die.

Marilyn probably will not miss me much. She's too pragmatic. Death is a natural culmination of life, she'll say, and the living have to go on living. I'm glad for that. I don't want to think of her feeling left behind, all alone in the world. Bucky will miss me a lot. Annie and Craig will miss me, a great deal more than they realize now. My sister Sissy will be sorry I'm no longer around for occasional visits but my older sister, Geri, who lives in California, won't miss me. Nita would have but she's too far removed now, as if in another life.

If my time on earth should be extended, this would be dear to me only in accord with the time I might yet spend with those I love. I want to see the grandchildren grow up and go to college. One of them might like poetry and study literature. There will be many changes in the world by then, but the words of Tennyson still will be beautiful and inspiring and whoever reads them still will find peace.

I know. I'm asking far too much. But isn't this why we dream? Unlike the dreams in our sleep, the dreams we have when we are awake are ours to craft as we will. It is through these dreams that we are able to create our world without regard to the way it is and see it as we would like it to be.

18 / Bucky

BUCKY GOT TO MEMORIAL Hospital at 4 a.m., after a two-hour drive south from Chicago on Interstate 57. He drove to the second level of a parking garage, where there were empty spaces near the elevator tower, and made his way to the hospital main building and through a long basement-level hallway to Wing C.

There were security guards on duty, but none challenged him and the first several doors were not locked. This struck him as somewhat ironic, as he had undergone an episode of intense questioning at the hands of a guard on exiting his own building in Chicago and again when he had to get his car. This place is wide open, he thought to himself. *But they go around the clock here, and I suppose working hours don't mean the same thing.*

The open-door policy ended abruptly when he got to Wing C. A sign on the door indicated that he needed an electronic pass of some kind to get in before 6 a.m. and directed him to a security phone on the wall in case of emergency. He stood for a moment, wondering what to do, and was about to turn and go back the way he had come when a man in scrubs wearing Memorial Hospital identification rushed up and opened the door.

"I'm going to trust you have business inside or you wouldn't be here," the man said, holding the door for him. "Come on through while I have it open."

"Thank you very much," Bucky told him. "I promise you I'm okay."

The man waved off any further comment and rushed on toward the nearest elevator. Before Bucky could catch up, the elevator door closed and the arrows on the direction panel indicated the car was on its way up. Bucky waited for another door to open and took an elevator to the 6th floor and walked directly to Room 12 in the ICU.

Inside, he stepped close to the bed and put a hand on the patient's shoulder. The arm and shoulder were encased in casts and bandages so that there was no feeling of human contact.

"I'm back," he announced. "Looks like you're still here. Did you miss me, buddy?"

He stood for some time longer, still touching the patient's arm, but said nothing more. He was tired of sitting after his long drive, but eventually moved to the chair against the wall. The room was quiet and had only low-level night lighting.

"Marilyn thinks it's about all over," he said, speaking in the general direction of his comatose friend. "I try to hold out more hope, but it doesn't look very good. You and I have survived some tough times together. This isn't the way I expected it to end. By the way, the Cubs are looking pretty good this year. I think we would have enjoyed those games."

He stood again, and turned to look out the window. The modest skyline of the surrounding community was well lit and in the distance he could identify structures he believed to be on the campus of the University of Illinois. There was a scattering of towers marked by flashing red warning lights and he wondered which of them might be actual broadcast installations and which merely offered microwave connections essential to all the cell phones and other channels of communication in this high tech age.

It struck him that the world had become almost a fantasy land, in which billions of people counted on what surely must be a fragile web of digital links that probably could be lost in an instant. He recalled an Isaac Asimov short story about an ancient civilization in a distant galaxy where the stars shone but once in a thousand years. Their unexpected appearance caused great fear and led inhabitants to a tortuous bout of panicked destruction that virtually obliterated such technological advances as had been made since the last time this happened, so that the cycle began all over again.

Asimov understood numbers, Bucky thought to himself. *He recognized the impression a "thousand-year" time period would make on his readers, compared to some general expression like "centuries."* Then he laughed at himself, that he would have the audacity to offer an evaluation of any form of literature.

"I am about to get way out of my league here," he said, turning back to the side of the bed that dominated the room. "That's something you'd know about, but not me. I wonder if Asimov ever wrote poetry. You would know, and probably quote me a verse or two if he did."

It was becoming more apparent that time was running out for the man lying before him, though Bucky could not say exactly why. Perhaps there were changes in vital signs showing on the electronic monitors on the other side of the bed but these usually were turned off and he couldn't read them, anyway.

"I was just thinking about the only thing we ever disagreed on," he said softly. "I couldn't get with your poets and you didn't care for my science fiction. But like Marilyn says, at the very least we both learned to read somewhere along the way and you got out of the woods and I got out of gangland in Kansas City."

He paused, as if giving his friend time to respond.

"I was looking at all the communications stuff out there and thinking about how the whole world should be able to come together now and not have to have war any more, you know? Then I realized that half the communications in the world probably is military and more likely to be used in mass destruction than peacekeeping. Maybe that Asimov story isn't so far-fetched after all. Hey, I'm sorry. You don't know what I'm talking about."

He went back to the chair and settled himself comfortably and was asleep when a nurse came a half-hour later. She tried to move quietly and not disturb him, but he soon woke and greeted her with a quiet, "Good morning."

"And good morning to you, too," she said. "You been here all night?"

"Not really. What time is it now?"

"Coming up on six-thirty. My shift ends pretty soon. We have plenty of coffee at the nurses' station if you'd like some. On the house."

"Thanks. I'm good. I've already had enough coffee to float a battleship."

"Well, I can identify with you on that. This place runs on coffee. We probably could get by if they ran out of morphine or sterile bandages and all that, but if they ever run out of coffee they may as well shut old Memorial Hospital down."

Bucky didn't respond, and she continued, "Marilyn was here late last night. We have a hard time getting that woman to leave."

"I know. She will want to be here at his side as long as there is breath in his body."

"You seem pretty devoted, yourself."

"He and I go back a long way. We were in the war together."

"Vietnam?"

"Yes."

"My uncle was in Vietnam. He says it did terrible things to the men who were there, but I've never heard him say anything specific about what it did."

Again, Bucky did not reply. He was looking out the window again, into the distance. Outside, the day already was bright with morning sunshine. It occurred to him that it was perfect baseball weather in Chicago and he wished his best friend could get up and get dressed and set off with him for a Cubs game at Wrigley Field.

19 / *I saw a cannonball tree*

I WILL ALWAYS REMEMBER the gigantic tree just outside our window, which Uncle Dick said was a sweetgum. People complained about its gum balls, the little spiked seed pods it dropped all over the ground that could hurt your foot if you stepped on one, but it was beautiful in the fall when the leaves turned bright colors. On moonlit nights in the winter, when it was bare, its black skeleton looked like some monster reaching up for us with its curved branches and it honestly scared me sometimes when I was little.

But I found comfort in it when I got older. If I had a nightmare or even if I just had trouble sleeping I could look out the window and there it stood, an enduring tower of strength. Its permanence was like an anchor in the rough waters of an uncertain world, and I knew everything was all right. I probably never had heard of Robert Frost then, but now I understand his verse about the "tree at my window," that there must never be a curtain drawn "between you and me." He could have been writing about my sweetgum tree.

We lived on the second floor of a building that had a hardware store below. We had only two bedrooms, and my sisters and I slept in one and my mother and Grand-mama slept in the other.

I thought my mother was the prettiest woman in the world. Maybe all boys feel this way, I don't know. But she was truly beautiful. She had blond hair and blue eyes and everyone said she looked like a movie star. The movies I saw then were mostly cowboy movies and didn't have many women in them, and they were in black and white, which would have made it harder to see how pretty a movie star was. But I knew she was prettier than any of the ones I saw.

I remember seeing a war movie, too. It was about Uncle Dick's war. I can't tell you the name of it or who was in it, but it made war look almost like fun. Everyone was heroic and no one got hurt and it had more pretty French girls than enemy soldiers. I guess everybody left the theatre feeling good and probably wondered why war was supposed to be so terrible. I wish whoever made it could have spent one hour in Vietnam. But maybe it's better not to see a movie about real war and then go home and have nightmares.

Well, since then I've seen lots of movies. They were right. Mama could have held her own with the most gorgeous stars. She aged gracefully and was beautiful to the end. She also kept on working well past retirement age, though she did cut back on her hours at the all-night diner. I don't remember exactly how old she was when she died. Sissy or Geri would know, but I don't think I ever see them anymore.

Mama had lots of boyfriends. We never saw them and they usually didn't last long. With the hours she put in on two jobs, how could she have had much time for them? I think they got tired of sitting around the diner just to see her and then, by the time she got off work it was too late to do anything.

I remember only one boyfriend Mama was serious about. He was a man from Kentucky who stopped by the diner pretty often after he'd done business in town. My sisters were sure Mama was going to marry him, but something happened that broke them up. I remember my mother crying about it and Grandmama telling her it was okay and life is full of hard knocks and we just have to take the bitter with the sweet, and anyway it was better to find out now than later. I didn't know what there was to find out.

But I did know that losing him changed my mother. After that, she never seemed really happy anymore. My sisters whispered about it and my grandmother worried about it, but I suppose there was nothing anybody could do to fix things.

Mama was very proud when I joined the Army, even though she knew I probably would end up in Vietnam. Soldiers were heroes, she said, and I would be serving my country while a lot of boys my age would be nothing more than hoodlums. She expected me to be welcomed home when the war was over, like Uncle Dick. I think she knew better by the time my actual homecoming took place, but in the meantime I had been wounded and nearly died and gone through months of surgeries and rehabilitation and I think she was happy simply to have me home alive.

I'm glad she had the pleasure of seeing me in my uniform when I came home on leave after basic training. She wanted me to come sit in the diner and let everyone in town visit. I did, and it was the most outgoing thing I ever did in my entire life. I never would have done it without her. And it breaks my heart, now, to know she had to face those people later when they all knew I was no hero. I guess I tend to overlook her most of the time when I think about all the people I love who I have hurt, but she should be high on the list. I'm sorry, Mama. And even if I'm given a dozen more chances to try to make up for what I've done, I'll never be able to make it up to you. I'm so very, very sorry.

Marilyn liked my mother. The two of them acted more like sisters together, not in-laws. I think they were a lot alike and Marilyn always missed her sister. When my mother died Marilyn grieved over the loss as deeply as I did. Grandmama didn't live long enough after Marilyn came along for the two of them to get very well acquainted. I know Marilyn would have loved her, too, and I miss Grandmama a lot even to this day.

One night in Vietnam I dreamed the big sweetgum tree was outside my window. I almost cried when I woke and saw where I was, surrounded by jungle. The jungle was all bamboo and vines and brush so thick you could not see through it. The banyan trees were wild—lots of trunks and not much top—and I saw one of the notorious cannonball trees. In some areas there was a heavy canopy of treetops, but you never saw what was up there because you had to keep your head down and watch the ground in front of your feet.

The jungle was a nearly impenetrable wall in places, so thick with bamboo and whatever grew on the ground the Vietcong could be hiding five feet away and you'd never see them. Only once did we come across a stretch where Agent Orange had been used. Pretty bizarre, everything dead. But they couldn't rely on Agent Orange because any time they sprayed with it the heavy rain might wash it away before it had time to work.

The Army engineers had used their Rome Plows— bulldozers with special blades—and chainsaws to clear around the first base camp I spent any time in. I heard that somewhere in the area they had tried monstrous tree crushing machines that just ran over and flattened everything in sight, but they said these got stuck in the mud in the swamps and the guys running them were easy targets for VC rifles.

The jungle hid hideous things. We stumbled across decaying corpses so often it became almost routine. And one time there was a Huey that had crashed and burned and still held charred bodies. Lieutenant Wallace, who wasn't a chaplain but apparently had been a part-time minister in civilian life, called out a detail to retrieve the remains. He prayed over what was left of the corpses as they used shovels to put them in body bags.

I remember looking around at all the jungle overgrowth and trying to remember the trees in Uncle Dick's woods and wishing I could see a squirrel. But when I remember this now it reminds me how I used to think nobody could shoot squirrels and foxes like Uncle Dick talked about, least of all me. I don't think I could have— but I shot people.

Trees live a long time. Unless they cut it down, that old sweetgum tree might still be there. I wish I could go see. If I get out of here alive, I believe I will.

Marilyn said the Shawnee National Forest would be my kind of place, away from the tensions of the city. She was in favor of our move out of Chicago. I know it wasn't that she wanted this for herself, but she wanted it for me. She said I could spend my days among the trees just like back on Uncle Dick's farm.

The forest has been good for me, except maybe for one embarrassing learning experience. I'd never heard of a tupelo tree until I read that the native forest in the Cache River basin not too far from our new home was a mix of tupelo and ancient bald cypress. I should have read more, but I wanted to go look at them. If I had read more I would have learned that these trees grow in swamps. My time among the trees of the Cache River forests was brief. There was no jungle, but I never, ever want to see a swamp again.

I like the distance between places down in the Shawnee. One of the ironies of my accident is that driving at high speed on an interstate highway always has been soothing to me. It doesn't matter whether the traffic is heavy or light, or whether I'm actually going someplace and have a schedule to keep or only looking for a stretch of open road with no distractions and no state troopers with radar guns. I am in control and have confidence in both my machine and my ability as a driver.

This all began during my boyhood days when Uncle Dick taught me to drive in his old Ford pickup truck. I was nowhere near old enough to get a license, but country roads in southern Indiana didn't require one. I don't mean legally, but you weren't going to get caught. By the time I was thirteen years old I could drive like a pro. Mama would let me drive her old Plymouth out to Uncle Dick's farm, and she never questioned whether I went straight there or took a few miles of round-about back roads to vent my frustrations and calm my anxieties. I drove fast—meaning a death-defying forty miles an hour—when I was in that mood and I always felt better for it.

Fast driving still works for me today. You don't have to explain the Eagles' song, "Take it to the Limit." I understand it. But I'm a careful driver and there is no irony in the fact it was not my fast driving that led to the horrendous accident on Interstate 57. Someone else's, maybe, but not mine.

I guess there is irony if you look at the wreck simply as an event without reference to the cause. I got all smashed up doing something I like to do on my way to spend time with Bucky. Two positives meshed into a severe negative. I'll write it off as merely a nasty twist of fate, although I am sympathetic to someone else's view that it was the act of a vengeful God who got impatient and decided it was time to collect His due. But surely even a vengeful God would not have hurt others just to punish me.

I do not understand why God would be vengeful, anyway. But then I've never been a student of the Bible and I've never had a pastor I considered relevant, unless you count Chaplain Lewis in the war. I never belonged to a church membership. Anything I think I know about a vengeful God I learned at Grandmama's church when she took me with her on Sunday mornings when I was little. I liked going with her, even though I didn't pay much attention to church. It seemed to me like the preachers always were mad about something and talked a lot about hell and that didn't sound like a place I was interested in. But I liked the music.

Grandmama was easy on me. As long as I didn't misbehave in public I probably could have gotten away with just about anything. She never talked to me about things the preacher said and I don't think she cared whether I paid attention. She acted like she was proud of me, and I could tell it pleased her when the other women in the church noticed me and complimented her on her cute grandson.

I mostly avoid talking about my childhood. You do things as a kid you'd never want your own children to know, at least until they get old enough to realize it was foolish and maybe dangerous and not okay just because their daddy did it. I'm as guilty of this as any other parent, and part of it I can blame directly on Uncle Dick's and Grandmama's books. Huckleberry Finn and Tom Sawyer might very well have been the end of me before I even made it to my teens.

My friend Terry and I set out to make a raft, like Tom or Huck, and planned to sail off down the Ohio River to who knows where. The adventures Mark Twain conjured up were exciting to hear about and there was no reason we couldn't do the same thing. We scrounged up some old lumber and a couple of dead tree logs and a large branch that had fallen from a sycamore tree and lashed it all together with rope we liberated from Uncle Dick's tool shed and got it in the water.

You may know, there is a lot of barge traffic on the Ohio. Just as we were about to set sail, a string of loaded barges pushed by a powerful tug boat with its surging twin diesel engines came along and created waves that sank our raft before we could climb aboard and get ready to cast off. And probably saved our lives.

You are the first ever to hear my lone river yarn. Terry and I kept quiet about it. I'd like to think this was because we understood what a dumb thing we'd done, but it probably was only because we had failed. Uncle Dick would have laid down the law if he knew what we did.

I want to tell this story to Craig, who will be glad to know I once had a spirit of adventure he can understand and appreciate. And there are so many other things we haven't talked about. I wish I could see him now and have a long talk.

I feel whatever's left of me slipping away. I'm trying to hold on and just the thought of sitting down with Craig and Annie and catching up with what's happening in their lives makes me determined to survive, the same way thoughts of going home to Grandmama and Uncle Dick did during the war.

All I ask is a little more time to be with my children again. And I want to be a better grandfather. It's too late for me ever to do as much for my grandchildren as Grandmama and Uncle Dick did for me, but I want to do things they will remember me for. I'm sorry I did not recognize how important this is until now, when I am face-to-face with the very great danger of never getting that chance.

I find solace in some of my favorite lines from the works of Longfellow, who said nothing is too late until "the tired heart shall cease to palpitate."

I'm going to hang on and get through this. I thought I was going to die in the war, but I lived. I'm determined to survive this time, too. I have so much more to live for. Marilyn, the children, the grandchildren. I will do it for them.

20 / *Marty and Jan*

IT WAS MARTY'S IDEA, and even though Jan didn't think it was a particularly good one she decided to go along. She appreciated Marty's sense of humor, which helped lighten both the occasional tedium of the job and the ever-present weight of caring for patients suffering from illness or injury that caused them to end up in the hospital. Nursing, as an early clinical instructor often had advised her class, was not for the faint of heart.

"Don't say anything," Marty insisted. "Just do it by looking. Look concerned, and kind of give her a quick once over like you noticed something new or different."

Kendra walked up at that point, and Marty promptly followed her own instructions. She managed a quick expression of concern and glanced sideways at Kendra and then deliberately turned her head, as if wanting not to be caught looking. Kendra picked it up on cue.

"What?" She looked down at herself, anxiously surveying her own body all the way down to her feet. "Is something wrong?"

"Oh, no," Marty assured her. "Everything's fine. It's just that, you know, in the early months—"

"I've not put on extra weight!"

Marty clapped her hands. "You just proved a theory, girl. I told Jan when a woman gets pregnant she worries too much about her weight. That's the first thing you thought of, even when I didn't say anything."

"Well, you can take your damned theory and shove it, Marty. The way you looked at me I thought—"

"Hey, I didn't mean anything. I'm sorry, kid. It's just that, you know, we're all caught up in the baby-making thing with you and I bet Jan you already were worried about putting on too much weight, that's all. Look, I get silly sometimes. You know that. I'm sorry, okay?"

Kendra looked at Jan, as if seeking some assurance. Jan nodded and smiled.

"I know, Marty," Kendra said. "But sometimes you just have a funny way of going about things. I'm cool now, okay?"

"All right. Onward and upward," Jan said, trying to sound more upbeat than she really was. "Hey, this is Memorial Hospital! We have great medicine to practice. What's the floor report this morning? Usual full house?"

Kendra slid behind the nurses' station desk and looked over a flow chart of rooms on their floor. Only half the ICU beds were filled, she announced, but not to worry. They would be covering half the non-ICU rooms because one of the other nurses was out sick.

"Well, ain't we lucky!" Marty declared. "Far be it from our considerate management to let us have a lighter load for once. How long's it been since we got any help when the ICU was jammed with critical patients?"

"I knew you'd complain," Kendra told her. "But you're not really put out about it. If you ever didn't have a full load you'd be disappointed not to have enough to do to keep busy."

Jan wanted to get to Room 12, but she needed to stop first in Room 4. This was her only new patient, a teenaged boy, and when she got there Doctor Jon Wiley was at the young man's bedside. He had his back turned when she entered but raised a hand and waggled fingers in greeting.

"It's been a while," the doctor said.

"Doctor Willy! It *has* been a while."

"Well, you know they do everything they can to keep me out of sight. How ya been, Jan?"

"Good. So what's going on with this good-looking young man?"

The patient beamed and Doctor Wiley gave Jan a knowing look. She knew he had a solid reputation for working hard to avoid the almighty physician stereotype and make doctor-patient and doctor-nurse relationships less formal. All this began with his insistence that he be called Doctor Willy.

"His summer has been pretty nearly ruined by recurring bouts of diarrhea," he said. "He assures me he's had no adventures in exotic foreign lands, so we think we need to find out what's going on in there. They did a colonoscopy early on that didn't show anything, but unfortunately they didn't do any biopsies. I'm betting on microscopic colitis, but we can't treat it till we find it."

Jan addressed the patient directly. "Don't worry, nothing gets by Doctor Willy. He'll have you fixed up in no time so you can enjoy the rest of your summer."

"Of course when I was his age I might have made things up for an excuse to be cared for by all you pretty nurses," Doctor Wiley said. He winked at the boy, who looked to be both embarrassed and pleased by the attention. "But we'll have him out of here before he gets to be too much trouble. Okay with you, Evan?"

The patient grinned and nodded.

Jan was busy checking the boy's vital signs. Everything was normal except his pulse rate. "Your heart's beating a mile a minute," she told him. "Have you been out of bed running up and down the hall or something?"

The patient seemed unsure how to respond and looked to Doctor Wiley for guidance. The doctor took the cue and assured her there was nothing to be concerned about. "It's one of those familiar physical responses we see in young men unaccustomed to close hands-on contact with female doctors and nurses," he said, his tone quite serious. "I believe the medical term is 'puberty.' I'm sure you've seen it before."

Jan tried to extend the doctor's gravitas, though she found it hard not to laugh. "Indeed. Straight out of my first clinical experience," she said. "It caught me by surprise, because none of our instructors had mentioned it." She finished entering the new information in the bedside computer and was about to leave the room when Doctor Wiley put a hand on her arm.

"Bring me up to date on the situation at home," he said. "I heard your husband is one of those who'd be called up if the Air Guard unit is deployed. Is that true?"

Jan was stunned by his question. "How in the world did you know about that?" she responded.

"A lot of people are talking about it. When it comes to things like this, we're all family. I guess you haven't seen it yet, but the hospital administration put out a memo that called attention to the impact the potential Guard deployment would have on the whole community and especially the staff here at Memorial. Some of the pediatric nurses were discussing it and I heard one of them mention your name."

"Good grief! Next thing you know, they'll be putting out a gossip column or something. How is this everybody else's business?"

Doctor Wiley apparently had not anticipated a negative reaction.

"Hey, I'm sorry," he said. "I didn't mean anything like that. It's just that, you know, we're concerned about you. It just seems like a sacrifice you shouldn't have to make."

"Look, I didn't mean to over react. I'm sorry, Doctor Wiley. I'm grateful for your concern—and everybody else's. It just took me by surprise that everyone seems to know about it. I'm not looking for sympathy, but yes, Phil's about to be deployed and I hate it. I'm having a hard time with it. But it is what it is and I'm going to have to learn to deal with it."

"There'll be a few others on the Memorial Hospital staff in the same position, I suppose. I hate it, too, Jan. But I want you to know you have a lot of support. Like I said, when it comes to things like this we are all family. I really mean that. If there's ever anything I can do please don't hesitate to let me know. Okay?"

Jan could feel the tears about to well up in her eyes. She never actually had thought about there being any common interest among the hundreds of hospital staff members beyond such things as salaries and working conditions and a general commitment to providing good medical care for patients. The group was too large, too diverse. Had she overlooked something that was there all along, or was the Air Guard deployment that big a deal that it tapped into something more?

Doctor Wiley answered her question, as if she had asked it aloud.

"I think there's something about this being a military action that makes people feel involved," he said. "I was in college when the Vietnam war protests reached their peak after the Kent State stuff in 1970. It wasn't that everyone knew somebody personally who was in the war, but it became an issue of national character or something like that. The military represents the whole country and everyone feels entitled to have an opinion on what it does, I guess. Am I making any sense?"

"Doctor Willy, you just explained it perfectly. You make me feel a lot better. Thank you!"

And she did feel better. The doctor's statement had struck a positive chord. Phil's absence would be no less painful, but she would not be facing this loss alone. Her husband would be serving his country and everyone in the community could rightfully claim a share in his sacrifice. She might be treading an uncertain path new to her, but it was a path countless wives had trod before.

And it is not only the wives, she thought. *Mothers and fathers and brothers and sisters and grandparents—whole families have watched their young men go off to war for generations.* She thought about how Emmie and the boys would miss their father, and her spirits sank again.

121

As she walked toward Room 12, Jan saw Marilyn and Bucky standing in the hallway just outside the door. Marilyn's back was turned, but Bucky saw her coming and stepped aside. She put a hand on Marilyn's arm and greeted them cautiously, afraid there might be bad news.

"Doctor Morrison is in there now," Marilyn said. "They took some new x-rays. There doesn't seem to be anything much different. We just needed to get out and stretch a little.."

When she went in, the doctor was studying the bed-side computer screen. "You're late," he said. "Or else I'm early. Good morning, Janet."

"Good morning, doctor. Anything new?"

"Yes and no. I had him back in radiology yesterday and just now saw the report. There's more damage to the left rib cage than we saw before. We knew there were four open fractures and some general caving up top, but there looks to be puncture signs we missed. If there is any deflation it's been minor so far, but I think there's real danger it will collapse. I just hate to try to go in and fix it right now."

"You don't think there's any point in that, right?"

"Your words, Jan, not mine. I've already brought his wife up to date on this, without the sharp edges. Sometimes the details aren't necessary. Agreed?"

"Agreed. You know how I feel about that."

As soon as Doctor Morrison left the room, Marilyn and Bucky returned. Jan was updating vital signs and checking the radiology report and new attending physician notes on the computer. She deliberately worked slowly, not eager to face Marilyn again after seeing the new x-ray reports and Doctor Morrison's notes. He had soft-pedaled the news, even to her. When she did turn to face the patient's wife and his best friend, she tried not to show a discouraging front.

"It looks like we're in for a hot one today," she said. Small talk avoided what she didn't want to talk about.

Bucky took it from there. Jan suspected he understood what was going on.

"It is summertime, after all," he said. "I guess we can't complain too much about hot weather."

"Phil says we all want cool weather in the summer and warm weather in the winter."

"I'm afraid he has that about right," Marilyn said. "And speaking of Phil, when's he due home now?"

Jan quickly felt more at ease. Small talk had saved her from facing painful questions about the patient. She told them Phil was scheduled to be home in two days, but it could be as early as tomorrow. His Air Guard unit didn't have to convoy with the regular Guard battalions' heavy vehicles.

"Just tell him he hasn't missed much by not getting in the real thing," Bucky said. "I guess it might not make as much difference from the air, though. If I ever had to go to war again that's the way I would want to do it."

Marilyn was looking past her, toward the door. Her face suddenly lit with excitement. "Annie!" she cried. "Oh, dear God, I'm glad you're here."

21 / *I worry too much*

I DON'T BELIEVE ANYONE could get much lower and more confused than I am right now. I can't seem to get my mental files in order and bunch together what is real separately from what feels real but may not be. But I can never give up.

I'm like the voice in that old rock song, "Carry On." I don't remember who did it. I was drunk the first time I

123

heard it and it really struck home. If you don't know it, the message is pretty simple. No matter what condition you find yourself in, you have to carry on. This became a dictum I lived by, but I'm no longer confident I have this drive within me.

It is the images that bother me most. I see Annie as a child alongside Annie as a woman, and Marilyn is explaining what it means to be a parent. I don't know if Marilyn is talking to me, but what she says is important. She knows what she's talking about.

Marilyn was a good mother. She still is, but I am thinking about before the kids left home. She could have written an advice column for parents or hosted a television talk show on raising children. Knowing the right thing to do always came easy for her. I'm grateful for this. If your child has a crisis you need to be decisive and they couldn't depend on me. I was too unsure of myself, afraid I might do the wrong thing, and so at times I did nothing. She always was there for them.

Oh, it was Crosby, Stills, Nash, and Young. I think that's who did the song. This may not be important and I don't need to worry about it.

Marilyn says I worry too much about everything. She says this out of concern for me, not in a way that casts blame. I'm grateful to her for that.

I wish I didn't worry so much. And I've tried not to. In the war they wanted us not to worry about collateral damage. You probably know, that is military talk for innocents suffering from the unintended consequences of something we did. It's the kind of language you hear from the command structure—the higher ups who make all the decisions. We weren't supposed to ask questions.

The higher ups apparently felt that collateral damage was something to be expected, and I don't think it was important to them. We had a mission, they said, and we were setting people free. We had a duty to God and country to focus on the mission.

I guess we were supposed to believe everyone would know our mission was good and be thankful to us for what we intended to do and accept collateral damage as part of the price they had to pay. There were some really gung ho guys in my company—including the company commander—and it may have worked for them, but it only made me worry more. I'd seen enough of our mission to know it was pretty uncertain.

I don't know how to explain this except to say I had a tough time seeing our mission as all good when they kept reminding us we were trained killers and it was hard to pick out anyone so bad that killing them seemed justified. And the more I thought about this, the more I wondered whether killing another human being ever could be justified. War is about killing and I came to question war itself and, especially, why I was in one.

As far as collateral damage was concerned, I was too hung up on questioning our mission to think much about it. I had no idea yet how truly horrendous collateral damage could be, but I would find out soon enough.

Like everything else, any mission's validity may just be a matter of perspective. Like Uncle Dick used to say: "It all depends on how you look at it, boy." If I had been shot by a Vietcong soldier, he would have been carrying out his mission and just doing his job. If he believed in his mission he would have felt good about killing me.

I was hit only a couple of days after we did the unspeakable thing we did to that pitiful, remote village. In a way, my wounds were merciful; they blocked from my mind, temporarily, the memories of that day. But the memories returned in time, and there's been hardly a conscious hour since when I didn't suffer wrenching guilt for our horrible deed. It comes back to me as if it is happening again, so that I must re-live it yet one more time. My squad is on point. There is a madding frenzy of rifle fire that sweeps through the streets of the village and beyond, extending to the dirt paths that offer the only hope of escape. We are not supposed to kill in-nocents, but we do. Collateral damage. The shooting that began as we approached the village just never stops, chewing away at everything in our path. We are trailed by the rest of our platoon and, to our flanks, the rest of the company. This is manifestly enough fire power to destroy life in a good-sized city, pushing through this compact collection of huts and outhouses like the winds of a hurricane. I wish it would stop here, but it doesn't.

I know this happened. I'm not sure when. I think it was several years ago. When I talk about it I begin to remember it better as I go along, a lot of the little details. It's like I was there right now. I think I was hurt again since then but I don't remember how.

I won't deny that I've suffered a lot physically from my war wounds. I don't feel pain now because of the morphine or whatever, but there is an odd feeling that could be because of the war or may be from whatever happened later. I don't know quite how to describe this, but somewhere in my midsection it feels like I'm being devoured by termites. It's not painful, but it worries me. I worry because I can't tell where the feeling is—whether it's somewhere in my belly or some vital organ, even whether it is in flesh or bone.

And I can't tell anyone. It may be important but the doctors don't know about it.

I think if I could talk I would be slurring my words. I feel the way I used to feel when Bucky and I had been drinking for an hour or so and the alcohol was beginning to make my brain a little foggy. I don't know what would make me feel like that now. Maybe the termites came from somebody's wine cellar. That's a joke. When I was teaching and talked myself into a hole during class I tried to joke my way out and my students liked the humor. I never was very clever at it, but sometimes it was good to lighten things up and help put the students more at ease. A teacher at college was a master of this and I always wished I was even half as good. I think it was Professor Sampson. I may have talked about him.

I was joking about termites, but if you think about it termites are very interesting. I guess their life cycles are predetermined. Maybe ours should be. Wouldn't it be easier, and save a lot of worry, if we knew there was a given time when our lifecycle would end? And we would know it was coming and plan for it and be ready, instead of acting like we thought we were going to live forever.

If I heard music now it would be The Byrds, "Turn! Turn! Turn!" You know, "To everything there is a season . . . ." Pete Seeger wrote the song and he took the words from the Bible, the book of Ecclesiastes. I don't think there is anything in the Bible about termites, but as I've already said I don't claim to be a Bible scholar.

I do confess to being guilty of anthropomorphism, lots of it, going back to my childhood. I didn't know what it was then, of course, but I talked a lot to the birds and squirrels and any stray dog or cat that happened by and just assumed they understood. It seemed to me we had a lot in common. I wondered if they were lonely like me, and if they welcomed our conversation as much as I did.

In high school, in Miss Lewellen's freshman English class, we had daily exercises in vocabulary. She insisted we learn one new word every day. That's where I learned "anthropomorphism." I still can quote the exact dictionary meaning: "The attribution of human traits to non-human things."

When Miss Lewellen gave us the meaning I thought she was looking right at me, like she could read my mind and knew I did it all the time. I didn't say anything, though, because the other kids would make a big deal out of it. "Talk to the rabbits today?" they'd say. They would taunt me endlessly about communicating with the animals better than I did with them.

Well, I could have told them the rabbits were better friends. The rabbits didn't make fun of the clothes I wore or my funny haircut or the fact that I didn't have a father. Teenagers get competitive and can be very cruel.

Before I met Bucky, and this was years later, the only close friend I ever had was Terry. Starting at about the fourth grade, Terry and I were like brothers and there is no way we could have been closer. My sisters stuck together and pretty much ignored me most of the time. They were open to me if I came to them with a problem, but that hardly ever happened. I would have died before admitting to them that anything was wrong if they didn't bring it up first.

I realize now that having a single mom and being raised by my grandmother and Uncle Dick was nothing out of the ordinary, even back then, but I didn't understand this at the time. I always pretended I had a father. I remember making up stories about my father the policeman and my father the truck driver and my father the soldier fighting a war somewhere on the other side of the world. I had a vivid imagination, and I put it to good use.

The truck driver was my favorite. My father could be on the road for days at a time, sending messages from exotic places like Colorado or Wyoming or the coast of California. I was good at geography. It was unlikely any of my young classmates would have caught an inconsistency, but I was careful not to have him in the East one day and far away on the other side of the Continental Divide the next. Big cities, mountain ranges, rivers, and state borders were my guide points and I learned them well. I knew all the states and where they were. Well, I think I got Vermont and New Hampshire mixed up at times, but I still do.

One of the reasons we all harbor subconscious desires to go back to being children again, I believe, is that when we were children we could let our imaginations run wild and pretend our imaginary world was real. If your father is a soldier fighting in a war far away, your friends don't question all your stories about his heroic actions and how he misses you and your mother and your sisters and can't wait to get home to see you again and probably will bring you exotic presents from wherever his war is taking place.

If you tell your stories often enough, you can almost come to believe they are true. When my father was a truck driver I told exciting stories about narrow escapes on winding highways through the Rocky Mountains and sometimes the other kids would get really interested. Terry knew I didn't have a father, but he never blew the whistle on me when I pretended I did. He would act like he believed my stories and wanted to know what happened.

Terry liked girls. He was in love with my mother, and later with my oldest sister, Geri. And one of the bigger thrills we enjoyed together was hiding in a closet and peeping through a crack in the door while Geri undressed and got ready to take a shower. The forbidden sight of a naked female body stirs the hormones of young boys like nothing else.

The only time I ever wanted to punch Terry out was when he bragged about seeing my mom naked and wanted to tell me all about it. I came down on him really hard and he never mentioned it again. I may have overreacted out of guilt because I'd seen her naked, too, and knew I should not have the kinds of thoughts I had about my mother. She was beautiful, though, and any boy would have enjoyed seeing what I saw. I'm embarrassed to say, I tried to get a peek every chance I had and it got to be a pretty regular thing.

That image of my mother standing naked in the dim lamplight is clear in my mind even now. I know I said the images confuse me, but this one is real. I know these things happened. Yes, I was young, and I might offer the innocence of youth as an excuse. But there was nothing innocent about the things I imagined while I watched my mother and Geri. And, all those years later, I wouldn't have youth as an excuse for the excitement I found in watching Nita undress. It was almost like William Blake had some mystic preview of her when he said the nakedness of woman is the work of God. But I may just be using Blake as an excuse for my own weakness. My grandmother used to say, "Everybody else does it isn't an excuse when you know it's wrong."

The world would be much less complicated if simply peeping on your mother or your big sister naked was the extent of damage from sexual desire. Why is the drive to reproduce so strongly embedded in every living organism? I'm not trained in biology, but it seems to me this is the most common factor visible in the entire natural world of living things. Plants and animals. Rocks aren't alive and don't reproduce.

I don't really know what became of Terry. His family moved to somewhere in Ohio when we were in the seventh grade. His father got a job in a steel mill, I think it was, and Terry said they were going to have a lot of money. I got tired of hearing that, but I hope they did and I hope Terry turned out well. He was a good kid.

Thinking about those years, when Terry and I were always together, brings a lot of pleasant memories. I'd be happy to go back in time, to have nothing more serious to worry about than to be caught peeping on naked sisters and never have to grow up. But maybe growing up wouldn't be so bad if you don't have to go to war. I wonder if Terry had to go to war, and if he did whether he got out of it without all the hurts Bucky and I got.

If I could go back in time I'd be content to sit on Grandmama's lap all day and listen to her read the poems. I think I could use some more time alone in the woods, too. I would have a happy life.

But we can't go back. Lying before us is Longfellow's shadowy future, which he said we should go forth to meet "without fear, and with a manly heart." I know

now that what I've told you was real, though, and as long as there are living memories the future is indelibly stamped by the past. Maybe I'll go to a book store when I get out of here and buy a thick volume of Tennyson poetry. Then I will go to the Garden of the Gods back in the Shawnee and sit on a rock in some sunny spot and read poems all day. And I'll look out over the valley below and watch the eagles soar over the forest and marvel at how much beauty there is in the world and be glad I got to see it one more time.

22 /*Annie*

ANNIE RAN AND THREW herself into her mother's arms and began to cry, softly at first and then in violent sobs. Jan and Bucky stood by awkwardly. Marilyn held her daughter and let her emotional outpouring run its course before saying anything more, waiting for Annie to speak.

"Mama, I'm sorry it took me so long. I'm not teaching in the summer session, but I had advising appointments and there's nobody to help. And then it was a long drive. Bryan and the kids will get here Saturday."

"Oh, honey, I'm just glad you made it," Marilyn said. "I need you here."

"Is Daddy any better?"

"Annie, he's not going to get any better. I'm sorry. His doctor says it's a miracle he's lasted this long."

Annie turned and leaned over the bed rail and kissed her father's bandaged head. She hesitated, looking for a place to grasp a hand. There was none.

"I can't believe it," she said, looking down but talking to her mother. "I thought it was good for you to move down there and he seemed so happy with it. Who would have thought this could happen? Do they know what caused the wreck?"

"I don't know. I've not made any effort to keep up with anything since I got here. Bucky's here."

Annie turned and smiled at Bucky and Jan. Then she stepped toward Bucky and opened her arms and he embraced her with the same spirit her mother had shown.

"It's good to see you, Annie," Bucky said. "It's been a while."

Jan introduced herself, then asked to be excused. "I'm glad you have more company now," she whispered, touching Marilyn on the arm as she left.

Annie returned to the side of the bed and put a hand on her father's chest. She began to cry again, and Marilyn came and put an arm around her. Bucky waited a moment, then moved up close behind them and put his arms around both women.

"I just can't believe this is real," Annie said, speaking barely above a whisper. "If you'd tell me that is not Daddy lying there, I'd believe it. You know things like this happen, but not to him. Do Aunt Sissy and Aunt Geri know?"

"Yes. I called them both," Marilyn told her.

"I'm not even sure I know where Aunt Geri is now. I never liked her. Is Aunt Sissy still in the senior place in Indianapolis?"

"Nobody likes Aunt Geri! Maybe it's not fair for me to say so, but it's true. She's in San Diego. Victor wanted to stay close to the Marine base after he retired. I talked with her briefly and she asked us to keep her posted on your daddy's condition but I don't think she was all that much concerned."

Annie made a face. "She's never been concerned about anybody but herself. Was Aunt Sissy upset?"

"Yes. And she wants to come. But you know she can't get around very well now. She's moved out of her apartment into the assisted living section of that place. I had a good visit with her on the phone."

"I'm sorry you've had to carry this all by yourself, Mama."

"I'm just glad you're here now. Bucky's been a lot of support. I know Craig is on his way, but who knows how long it will take him to get here."

"Craig will do whatever it takes. And, Bucky, I know Daddy's happy to have you here at his side. With you two, that's kind of the natural order of things. And he was on his way to see you when the accident happened?"

Bucky said it was true, and expressed a sense of guilt. Both Annie and her mother told him it wasn't his fault and he must not feel guilty. Annie tried to make small talk about the Cubs and her surprise to hear that Bucky had gone back to work and how happy she was that her parents' move south had turned out well. Bucky said it sounded so good he had been thinking about moving down that way, himself.

Marilyn wanted to give Annie time alone with her father. She suggested to Bucky that they go to the coffee shop and get breakfast, and asked Annie to join them there later. On their way to the elevators, they met Jan.

"I was just on my way to give you some news," Jan said to Marilyn. "The little girl who was in the accident can have visitors now, if you're still interested. I can get her name and room number if you like."

"Please. I'd like to see her."

The three of them walked to the nurses' station and Jan spent a few minutes on the phone and computer before announcing she had the information. "Sometimes these things are routine and sometimes all I get is busy signals," she explained. "Things worked the way they are supposed to this time. If I needed to do it again ten minutes from now it might take all day."

"Is this a time I could visit?"

"They don't show any restrictions."

"Annie will be there with her dad for a while, so I think I'll go ahead and check in on her now. Thank you, Jan. Oh, what is her name, again?"

"Her name is Amy. She's fourteen."

"Want to go, Bucky?"

Bucky shook his head. "I have some things to take to the car," he replied. "How 'bout I catch you later in the coffee shop?"

"That'll work. I won't be long, and Annie probably will be down soon, too."

Marilyn thanked Jan again, then she and Bucky went to the elevators and she went up to the next floor. The layout, including room numbering, was the same and she went directly to Amy's room. A white privacy curtain was drawn around the bed, where a doctor was examining the patient. A woman sitting in a corner of the room looked up as she entered but didn't speak.

"I just wanted to check on Amy," Marilyn told her. "My husband was in the same accident she was hurt in and they told me it would be all right for me to visit."

The woman smiled. Marilyn could see that she was tired. "She likes to have visitors. The doctor will be done in a little while and you can see her."

"Are you her mother?"

"Yes. I'm sorry. Looks like I've forgotten my manners. I'm Deena Arnold, Amy's mother."

"I'm Marilyn. I know this is an ordeal, Mrs. Arnold. I'm sorry for what happened. Were you in the wreck?"

"No. She was riding with her grandparents. My in-laws."

A nurse opened the privacy curtain and pulled it around its frame to the wall, so that Amy no longer was hidden from view. The doctor gave his young patient a high-five and turned to her mother. "Everything looks great," he said. "She should be ready to go home in a couple of days." Then, after looking back at Amy and winking, "Of course, you probably aren't in any hurry to get this troublemaker back, anyway."

Amy's mother played along. "I might just let you keep her," she said. "But I expect she'll be glad to get out of your way."

The doctor nodded at Marilyn as he left the room. The nurse went to the bedside computer and began typing notes into Amy's file. Amy was all smiles for her mother, and raised a hand in greeting when told she had a visitor.

"It sounds like you got a good report," Marilyn said. "My name is Marilyn. My husband is here in this hospital, too, in the ICU. It sounds like you're doing well."

"Hi, Marilyn. I'm good. Doctor Daffy says I can go home in a couple of days." And, turning to her mother, "Did he tell you that?"

"Yes he did," Deena Arnold said. "I think he just wants to get rid of you. Wasn't it nice of Marilyn to drop in to check on you? Her husband was hurt in the same accident you were in."

Amy sobered. "I'm sorry. Is he going to be okay? I didn't know anybody else was hurt."

Marilyn hesitated, unsure what she should say and hoping the girl's mother would respond. She did.

"He was hurt worse than you," Deena Arnold told her daughter. "We just have to feel very lucky, don't you think? Doctor Daffy wants you to get some more sleep now, so Marilyn and I are going to go somewhere else to talk and not disturb you, okay? I'll be here when you wake up."

The girl agreed and thanked Marilyn for coming. Marilyn congratulated her for being such a good patient and making a speedy recovery. The two women went to a nearby family lounge and Deena Arnold explained that her daughter had suffered cuts and bruises and a concussion and there hadn't been any complications.

"Her doctor wanted to keep her here a few days under observation as an extra precaution."

"Doctor Daffy? Is that his real name?"

"No. He's Doctor Danielson. He wants the kids to call him Doctor Daffy for fun. They say that's something of a tradition among the pediatric doctors here. He's kind of a character. Amy just loves him."

"Your daughter is a real sweetie. I hope she doesn't have any complications. It's painful to see these things in kids."

"I didn't have a chance to tell you, but she doesn't know her grandparents were killed in the wreck. She asked about them when she was still kind of groggy and I couldn't bring myself to tell her the truth. She's going to have to know sooner or later, and she's going to be heartbroken."

"Oh, I'm sorry," Marilyn said. "Do you have someone to help with it, I mean—"

"Her father will do it. It was his parents who were killed, so he's pretty much crushed right now and has been tied up with his brothers and a sister making arrangements and all that. They were the sweetest old couple in the world. Amy was crazy about them."

"Look, this is none of my business, but I know how painful these things are on children, even under the best of circumstances. And on you, too. I have talked with counselors a lot because of my husband's war injuries and I see some parallels here. Amy may feel guilty that she survived and they lost their lives."

"I never thought about that, but it makes sense. Do you have any advice?"

"I'm in way over my head here, Mrs. Arnold, but—"

"Please. Call me Deena."

"Yes. Deena. I'd be afraid any advice I had might be wrong. Maybe your minister, or—"

"I guess I didn't tell you. My father-in-law was our minister. We've a whole church full mourning their loss.

And he was wonderful at counseling on things like this. He and my mother-in-law started out as missionaries in the Philippines when they were a young couple and worked there for years. Then he—well, both of them— got really involved in the anti-war protests during Vietnam and they never went back. Back to the Philippines, I mean."

Marilyn shook her head sadly. "I'm so sorry for your loss. We just jumped right into things in the beginning so I didn't get a chance even to find out where you folks are from or anything like that."

"We live in St. Louis."

"Did your in-laws live there, too?"

"Yes. Their church—I should say, our church—is on the west side, just outside Clayton if you know St. Louis. But tell me about your husband. Was he seriously hurt?"

"He's critical. We don't think he's going to make it."

Deena Arnold's face expressed both her surprise and her instant sympathy. She spoke the appropriate words, as well, and then there was little more to say. She thank- -ed Marilyn for her concern for Amy and asked to be informed of any new turn of events. It went without saying that this meant the death of Marilyn's husband. Marilyn, in turn, repeated her regrets over the Arnold family's loss and her pleasure in finding young Amy doing well.

As they parted company, they both knew they had been brought together by merest chance through one tragic event and their paths were not apt to cross again. And yet this short time together left two families sharing a sense of enduring pain and a keen realization that life is fragile and must never be taken for granted.

23 / *I knew war*

I REMEMBER THE HELPLESS feeling I had for a couple of days after the first surgery I went through in the war, but it was nothing compared to the way I feel now. My body was just as useless then, but I could see and hear what was going on. I could talk and let the doctors and medics know if something didn't seem right and they usually could explain things in a way I could understand. They were generous with drugs that kept me from feeling pain.

Right now I feel bugs crawling on my skin and I know there probably aren't any bugs on me but I can't tell anyone and have them look and be sure. I would like to scream for attention, but I can't do that, either. There could be a doctor standing over me but I can't tell. I am alive in my own mind, but it seems to me that without functioning senses my mind would be operating only on accumulated memory. This may not fit with what you'd read in the medical text books, but I've never read a medical text book and this is what I believe.

I think something sharp and metal pierced my body in the accident, but maybe it was in the war. It is an imprecise memory. It may have been bullets. Bullets tear through flesh and bone as if there is no resistance, yet the shock is like being hit by a massive force crushing the whole body and stunning the senses like a blow to the head.

And God help us, we did this to innocent people who would have done us no harm. I know this is true.

But I'm calling on God again, like I believed there was one in control of earthly beings and I don't. A god who cares about every little sparrow would care about babies in their mothers' arms and old people who were not hurting anybody and not leave them lying in a ditch riddled with bullets. A god who cares would have stopped the war and ended the killing.

I know I talk about "the war" like Vietnam was the big one everybody will always remember, and I know this isn't true. Vietnam probably is long forgotten by most people and its marginal space in the history books has all but disappeared. New generations will barely know it happened, much less understand the long national trauma it brought on our nation. But for me—and I know Bucky feels the same way—it is *the war* because it stole our youth and innocence and left us damaged in ways we still have not been able to come to grips with.

Like I said when I was talking about Terry, sometimes I try to think what it would be like to be able to go back in time and live parts of our lives over again. I saw this in a movie many years ago. I don't remember the movie very well, but I believe it wasn't very interesting because the character hadn't done anything he was especially desperate to change. He had a different romance and became an artist instead of a banker or something like that. That's not what I'm talking about. I'm talking about getting a new life that doesn't include being in war.

Uncle Dick always acted like he was proud of being in World War II, the big war, and I've known some other older guys who were in it who seemed to feel the same way. They no doubt saw plenty of death and destruction, too, but apparently were able to put all this behind them and get on with their lives.

Uncle Dick never mentioned nightmares about being in battle. I know this doesn't necessarily mean he didn't have them. One of my counselors at Indiana State who worked with a lot of us Vietnam guys said many of the men who fought in World War II had the same nightmares we do, but hardly anyone ever talked about it.

This counselor tried to draw a distinction between being in combat and being in war, which I didn't follow at the time but understand a little better now. Combat, or battle, would scar anybody, he said, and that's where the nightmares come from. But *war* is something a lot broader.

Insofar as combat is concerned, he said infantrymen fighting on the ground in Uncle Dick's war didn't spend nearly as many long stretches as we did in actual battle without a break, and this is a big part of what makes it feel like you're never going to get out alive. And when you spend so much time in combat it is even more likely to make an indelible impression on your brain and show up over and over in nightmares for years to come.

The counselor said war leaves a lot of death and destruction even if it's justified, but the men in World War II felt like heroes because they knew everyone at home was behind them and indebted to them for serving. Hardly anyone doubted theirs was a war that needed to be fought. But we didn't get this, and if you are led to believe what you did was not heroic you are likely to believe it was wrong and feel guilty. It wasn't like we were over there tending the sick or feeding the hungry, after all. We were there to kill people.

I liked this counselor a lot, and I think he knew what he was talking about. He helped me understand some important things about what I had done. I still might argue one point with him, though. He said we can't claim our war was harder because we'd never been in a jungle before, when the World War II guys who were in the Pacific fought in jungles just like we did.

Okay, but Uncle Dick was in Europe and his war left him with stories about pretty French girls and bottles of wine in bombed-out farm houses and all that. But then, as the counselor would have pointed out, Uncle Dick was not in the Pacific. For all I know, France may have been like Indiana.

I went to war as a naíve, easily duped teenager with no clue what I was about to get into and totally un-prepared for the horrible things that happened. Most of the other guys in my unit were just kids, like me. I don't think anybody in my rifle squad was over twenty. We were exactly what the military wants, of course, because unsuspecting teenagers are not likely to ask questions. They just follow orders.

"Charge of the Light Brigade" was among the works in Grandmama's little book of Tennyson poems, and was among her favorites. I knew the words and subcon-sciously subscribed to the message: "Theirs not to reason why, Theirs but to do and die." In other words, I was potentially the loyal, gung ho soldier the Army wanted me to be. And the pride I took in that uniform made it hard for me to take issue with what I was called on to do.

This didn't last long. I've already told you, I found the emphasis on killing hard to justify. I was not ready to accept collateral damage as routine. In the end I was as guilty as all the rest, but not because I had changed my mind about our mission and decided what we were doing was good. There were no noble intentions leading to what I did.

This may be a cowardly validation, but in a fire fight in a remote village in a part of the world entirely alien you do what everybody else is doing. You are about to die and you as an individual don't matter. Your infantry company is a killing machine that will sweep through whatever lies before it and few people ever will know and even fewer ever care. That's the way it felt at the time.

But even Bucky, who saw more war than I did, can-not understand how we did what we did that day. He has never blamed me, though, and he never mentions the worst of what he knows to be true.

You understand, I didn't know Bucky until after we both had been wounded and ended up undergoing some of the same medical treatment. We were in combat in the same general area, but our paths never would have crossed except for getting hit. He used to joke that getting your body riddled by bullets was a high price to pay for a lifelong friendship. And then he'd always turn serious and say he was glad it happened. Glad we met, I mean, not glad we both got shot up.

Bucky got his wounds, his physical wounds, a few weeks after I did. The wounds to his mind and spirit probably developed over time. He was in a lot more action than I was because he survived combat duty for almost a full year before he got hit. My third or fourth search-and-destroy mission turned out to be my last.

Time is supposed to ease the mind and make things go away, but when it comes to the war there are some ways in which time only has made things worse. The longer I've had to look back on it, the more cheated I feel that I had no chance to redeem myself for things I did in that first few months. Had I been in combat long enough, I might have done something good, something heroic. Or I might have been killed instead of only wounded, which from my current vantage point would seem just.

But much of life you don't control, and this is especially true in war. And I was too young, too innocent, too unaware of the ways of the world.

If I am about to face final judgment, though, I do so fully aware that being young and immature is no excuse. I knew what was happening was wrong. I did nothing to try to stop it. The things I did, myself, were bad enough, but I watched the terrible things other guys did without ever raising a hand or saying a word. And it was not because I was afraid or helpless, even though I might have been, but because at the time I didn't care. It was as if nothing mattered anymore.

I was a mature man when I did the other thing—the thing that hurt Bucky and would hurt him even more if he knew. I may have been swept along by circumstances in the war, but this time circumstances were largely of my own making. I saw it coming and had plenty of time to stop it before it went too far. I could have stopped it, but I didn't. I deserve all the torment it has caused me, but the others don't. How can I expect their forgiveness, even if I live to ask for it?

Am I paying now for my transgressions? My mind is alert and active, but I cannot communicate even a simple thought. I cannot raise a finger to signal that I am alive. The terror I feel thinking I might lie here for days or even weeks or months in this condition is as great as any terror I ever faced in the war or the shadowy world of the unknown I fell into later, trying to find liberation in drugs and alcohol.

Is this my punishment? Would it have been merciful to have been road kill on that busy interstate highway like the flattened raccoon or coyote smashed into oblivion on contact? Is it given that I am not permitted quick escape from the menacing world like I would have been by a bullet through my heart or head in the war? Am I destined to suffer longer, face my demons again and again and know they are much more powerful than I and understand there is no escape? Are they to eat away my life a nibble at a time and laugh in my face like a schoolyard bully?

Shakespeare wrote that cowards die many times before their deaths, and only the valiant taste of death but once. I have died those cowardly deaths in spirit because I am ashamed of things I've done, yet I never have asked anyone for forgiveness.

24 / *Bucky and Annie*

BUCKY WAS WAITING when Marilyn got to the coffee shop, and Annie joined them a few minutes later. Bucky greeted Annie with a hug and the two of them exchanged updates while Marilyn stood and stretched. Bucky said Annie never aged, and still looked like a teenager. Annie laughed, but made little effort to hide the pleasure she took in his compliment.

"And you're still married to the same dull guy and spend your time trying to teach college students who'd rather be at some sleazy bar drinking beer and all the other routine stuff that was going on the last time I saw you?" he teased.

"Well, yeah," Annie said. "My life has all the drama of a thunderstorm in July. So what's going on with you these days, Bucky? Besides going back to work, I mean."

Bucky threw up his hands, as if in a surrender movement. "So little that a July thunderstorm sounds pretty exciting."

"I'm sorry it took what it did to bring us together. It's just so hard to see Daddy lying there, and thinking of all the things I wanted to tell him about and know I can't do it now. Do you really think there's any hope?"

"We can never give up hope. That's all we have."

Marilyn pulled out her chair to sit back down. "I guess I need to update you on what I said earlier," she told Annie. "Aunt Sissy is on her way. She called while I was on my way down just now."

"Really? I didn't think there was much of a chance of that. I'm surprised she can make the trip."

Bucky said he was surprised, too, but happy to hear the news. "Sissy was always his favorite," he said. "And it shouldn't be too hard for her to get here from Indianapolis. How's she making the trip?"

"The son—no, the grandson—of one of her friends is going to drive her. She said he went to school here and has made the trip about a million times."

"I had forgotten about the university being here," Annie said. "You can't drive into town without knowing it, though. That's a big campus."

Bucky's face suddenly lit up with a wide smile. "This is where we came to the Dylan concerts and your mom and dad came for that big Willie Nelson thing in the football stadium," he said. "I know she remembers that."

"Farm Aid," Marilyn said. "The first one. I think they are still going on. It was a great concert. You watched it on television and I'll bet you remember the shocking news the broadcast made, too. We thought it didn't get on the air, but—"

Annie interrupted. "Wait, wait now. What shocking news? I don't remember hearing about this."

"That's because it wasn't something for the tender ears of a child like you were at the time," Bucky said. "Now that you're all grown up, and a college professor, even, I guess you can hear it. Keep in mind that it was broadcast live over the Nashville Network—"

This time it was Marilyn who interrupted. "It would not have mattered. We didn't have all the cable networks then and the censorship standards were a lot tougher. But go ahead and tell her."

"Well, that's exactly right. I think they had a ten-second delay or something, but they were kind of caught off guard and somebody didn't push the button in time. So all those good Southern kids listening to Willie and John Mellencamp and Dylan and Neil Young and Tom Petty and the Beach Boys and a slew of other big-name performers heard colorful language they didn't normally get over the old Nashville Network. One of the rock group front men was announcing their next number and dedicated their performance to 'all you motherfucking tractor jockeys out there,' which made it onto the airwaves."

"You're kidding!" Annie exclaimed. "I doubt this even would raise any eyebrows now, but it probably was pretty shocking back then."

"Sad but true," her mother said. "I'm not a prude, but I don't think the relaxed standards of cable television and the Internet have improved communication much. Sometimes the language is just distracting."

"What does Daddy think about that? He loves the language so."

"It's hard to tell. I only remember him saying 'ugly' language would never have the staying power of Tennyson. But you know your father. If it doesn't glorify war or violence he doesn't criticize it. He always says there's lots of different fishes in the sea and lots of different trees in the forests so we have to allow for diversity in everything."

"Oh, yes! How many times have I heard that? Uncle Dick, right?"

"He learned a lot from Uncle Dick."

Bucky was about to speak when Marilyn held up a hand, indicating she wanted silence. "Wait," she said, "I want to hear this."

A newscast was in progress on the television set on the opposite wall, above their heads, in the middle of a report from St. Louis: ". . . say the Arnolds were well known, even beyond their congregation, for their years of anti-war activism. The minister was among those injured at Kent State University in 1970 when the Ohio National Guard fired on protesting students. He was not hit by gunfire, but suffered facial cuts from flying glass. Funeral services . . . ."

"Someone you know?"

"Not really. But I know who they are. It's a small world, Bucky."

25 / *I hear the music*

I THINK THEY ARE doing something to me now, but I can't tell what. I sense motion. I am not moving, so somebody else probably is. I may not be in Vietnam. I know I was. They sent me to Charlie Company, which was already there. Yes, Greer and I both were in Charlie Company because they needed us to take the places of guys that had been killed. We were supposed to kill other people but not be killed ourselves and they always made sure we had lots of bullets.

I remember Annie talking about balance in nature. She would have noticed how the Army maintained balance with its big Hueys that hauled bullets in and bodies out. Body bags have six handles and are closed by a zipper. I don't know how many filled body bags a Huey could carry. When a soldier is killed his body is treated with great respect. Annie would have hated the Army version of balance. Annie wouldn't kill anything.

I don't want to think any more about body bags. I want to hear music. Any music. I remember Bucky saying the mandolin never could make real music, then we heard and loved Rod Stewart's "Mandolin Wind." I wish I could hear it now, summon it up in my senses and make it truth and light and beauty and be surrounded by it and let it become my universe.

I think they sang "Amazing Grace" every Sunday at Grandmama's church. I always tried to join the singing to please her, and I learned most of the words. Repetition will do that. I thought the words were beautiful and eventually I came to understand what the song meant. Of course, I didn't know then that John Newton, the man who wrote it, had been a slave trader after he got out of the British Navy and turned to God for help after his ship was endangered during a storm. All this is something I learned from Marilyn.

Has there ever existed a single human being who didn't feel cheated at some point in life when they found out that something they'd been taught was not real, but actually a fraudulent illusion? Santa Claus? The Easter Bunny? Tooth Fairy? Prince Charming? Pot of gold? War to end all wars? War on drugs? You'll feel better in the morning? It'll only hurt for a minute? You'll look back on this someday and laugh? The lieutenant knows what he's doing? Peace in our time? It tastes like chicken?

Okay, I wish I could be less cynical. But actually, I'd be inclined to add another illusion to the list: God is good. I've seen too many bad things in this world, which God is supposed to be in control of. Or maybe when people say this they mean God is good because they truly believe in redemption. If John Newton could count on the grace of God getting him into heaven after carrying shiploads of human beings in chains to be sold for slaves, he had a lot more faith than I do. I assume he truly believed that all he had to do was ask. Did he expect to see the faces of any of those black Africans among those welcoming him to paradise?

Was it the mere thought that leads me to hear Newton's hymn in my head now? Why do I keep hearing music? I've been trying to figure that out, and I think I may have an answer.

There has to be an immense accumulation of things stored away in our brain—facts, memories, emotions, visual images, and other things we have experienced through our senses, all the things from the first words we learned to the taste of chocolate and complex patterns of information ready to be strung together when we need them so we don't have to go learn them all over again. You remember how to read when you pick up a book, no matter how long it has been since you first learned the alphabet. And then, if your head gets knocked around in a wreck or something like mine did and all these things get jumbled up together, you can't control your thought patterns and the electrons in your brain are misfiring all over the place and everything tries to pop up at once. This may not be scientific, but it is what I believe is going on.

I love music and I've listened to a lot of it. Just as I concentrate on the poems when I read Tennyson, I concentrate on the music when I listen, meaning it doesn't have much competition going on in my brain and it seems logical it would make an impression. At the very least, there surely are fragments of much of it stored away in my head and now they're trying to compete with everything else I've ever learned.

I've always thought of myself as a simple man. It's almost as if my closest brush with sophistication was trying to understand the meaning of Led Zeppelin songs like "What is and What Should Never Be" or how musicians can sing and play instruments at the same time and all blend together with such perfect timing the way the Eagles band does.

One song I did understand the first time I heard it was Pink Floyd's "Comfortably Numb." If you know it, I don't have to explain, and if you don't and I tried to explain I probably would make it sound like something bad when it isn't. It's about pain and loneliness and needing help to face life and feeling the difference between life as it should be and life propped up by drugs or alcohol or whatever, the way I was. I felt the message then and wallowed in the angst David Gilmour wrings from the strings of his guitar, and I still do.

David Gilmour and I probably are about the same age. I wonder, did he ever have to go to war? If he had been wounded like Bucky and I were, could he still have played his music? I would like to sit and talk with him, tell him about the times his music has kept me afloat in a perilous universe where everything else was sinking. Or, I might be speechless, like a star-struck teenager.

Tennyson says music is gentler on the spirit than eyelids on tired eyes, but he wasn't talking about the kind of music Bucky and I came to lean on. You probably wouldn't consider rock music gentle. But gentle or not, music can be an escape from reality. This is what we wanted and needed, and this is the reason music helped us through the toughest of times. I'm guessing the same might be said for John Newton.

Not to try and make too much of this, but I think the music most of us identify with is the music that fit our needs at a given point in life. The simple tunes we learned as kids take us back to a time we were innocent and unsuspecting about the real world we were yet to enter. The patriotic songs we sang in school taught us to love our country. We re-live the emotional years of adolescence through the romantic songs we listened to then, and for those in my era the rock music and protest lyrics marked our young adulthood. John Lennon's "Give Peace a Chance" was an honest plea fitting to its time. We remember the music because we want to, and the music we choose to remember may be nothing more than the music that helps block out things we want to forget.

I still wish sometimes I had been the rock guitarist I hoped to become when I was young. If I had been, I could look back on a lifetime offering escape to millions who heard my music, maybe turning to it in their darkest hours the way I did David Gilmour's.

The modest contribution I made as a teacher was the best I could offer. My own words were inadequate, but I used the words of Tennyson and other great poets the way I would have used the compositions of others had I been a musician. Students didn't flock to my classroom the way they would have to a Pink Floyd concert; they came to my classroom because they had to. But some, at least, went away better for the experience. I need to believe this. I need to think I helped my students learn to value words and find ways to make words into meaning that connected them better to a wider human universe.

I hope I taught them that words, used well, become poetry. And I tried to show how poetry becomes music.

Longfellow said music is the universal language and poetry is the universal delight. But most teenagers in the throes of coming of age care nothing of Shakespeare's Romeo and Juliet, nor Tennyson's spot-on observation that, "Never morning wore to evening, but some heart did break." But they feel the Eagles' "Heartache Tonight" and "New Kid on the Block." If writers seek to be poets, poets seek to be musicians. This is what I believe.

Marilyn says Neil Diamond's soft rock lyrics come closest to poetry, and explain how he connects with listeners even more through his words than through his music. I'd never thought of it until she pointed out the subtle difference between Brooklyn *Roads*, in his song by that name, and Brooklyn *streets*.

"Streets get you around town," she said, "but roads take you home." For one who prefers to work with science, Marilyn is very good with words.

But I do not pretend that I have seriously affected young lives. I am not a poet, and I am not a musician. In the words of Keats—ah, yes, how easily I steal from the masters!—my teacher's epitaph will be, "Here lies one whose name was writ in water." When the water dries, my name will disappear and I soon will be forgotten.

Or even more fitting, not because I was a teacher but because of what I did in the war, would be the fate so aptly put by Tennyson, "The years will roll into the centuries, And mine will ever be a name of scorn."

I want to hear "Amazing Grace" again. I want to sing the words, to know Grandmama is proud of me. Like the slave trader who wrote it, I want to believe that grace brought us safe thus far, and grace will lead us home. I want to, but such blind faith is not within me. I'm sorry, Grandmama.

I believe I hear it. No, it is the mandolins. Let me hear them and listen and not think about the war and Greer, and trying to stop the blood but knowing it was too late. They didn't even do a dustoff call for Greer. Chaplain Lewis said a prayer over him but he didn't hear it. Chaplain Lewis said Greer was being welcomed in heaven and I wondered if he would be put back together again when he got there or whether arms or legs made any difference in heaven.

But I am listening to the music now. I will not think about those other things. I will put it all aside and listen. And listen. Listen. The music is soothing. This is the gentle music Tennyson talked about. The humble mandolin makes sweet music. I like the throbbing guitars but the mandolin is soothing. I will listen to the mandolins.

26 / Jan

J AN WAS TIRED, after a near-sleepless night. Though her spirits had improved somewhat after her conversation with Doctor Wiley, she had slipped back into the old level of anxiety over Phil's deployment and had spent much of the night mentally running through all the ways she had thought of in which his absence might make life worse for her and the children.

The bottom line simply was that they would miss him terribly. But this was a given; there were practical, quantifiable difficulties his absence would lead to and she wanted to be prepared.

Phil's mother had tried to brighten her mood, and even persuaded her there still was some small chance the Guard unit's deployment wouldn't happen. It was, at this point, still only a rumor.

She tried to put on a happy face as she approached the ICU nurses' station. Marty wasn't there yet. Kendra actually ran to meet her, obviously excited.

"I found out what's going on," she called as Jan got close. "Mark told me everything last night."

Jan was hesitant for an instant, because deep down she was afraid to hear what Kendra was about to tell her. But she tried not to let this show. "So tell me, quick!"

"He's been gambling and he has lost a lot of money. He says—"

"Gambling? Where? I didn't know there was any place around here where you could gamble."

"It's all on line. You know, on the Internet. Evidently there are a lot of sites where you can do it."

Jan felt a sense of relief. In her mind, she had gone over all the possible causes of Kendra's problem she could think of, and gambling was not one of them. It seemed less dangerous than most of those she had considered. It did not involve anyone else. Or did it?

"So this is not like shooting craps in some dark alley with hoodlums, right? No mob money involved? You're not going to wake up in the middle of the night and find a couple of men in black suits busting in with big guns demanding cash?"

Kendra was about to reply when the elevator door opened and Marty appeared. "I'll fill you in later," she whispered. "I don't want her to hear."

It was apparent immediately that Marty was not in her typical upbeat mood. The usual bright smile was missing. She walked straight to Jan and put a hand on her arm.

"I'm so sorry, honey," she said. "I just heard. Even though you knew it was coming, I know it's tough."

"Marty . . . what?"

"Oh, shit! You hadn't heard. Me and my damned big mouth!"

Kendra raised a hand to her face and made a sound somewhere between a gasp and a groan. "It's something new with the Guard, isn't it?" she demanded of Marty. "Did it just come out?"

"God, I'm sorry," Marty said. "Yes, it was just on the morning news. It's official. They are sending the Air Guard to Afghanistan, effective in ten days. I'm so sorry, Jan. Just smack me up side the face, okay?"

Jan felt a momentary surge of light-headedness, as if she were about to faint. She caught hold of the edge of the counter that surrounded the nurses' station to keep from falling. "I knew it was coming," was all she could think to say.

A short time later, in Room 12, she walked past the patient to the window and opened the blind so that sunlight streamed in. There was a steady flow of pedestrians in both directions between the hospital and the parking garage on that side of the building. She stood and watched the comings and goings below, leaning into the window with both hands on the marble sill. Who were all these people and what was going on in their lives today? Did any of them have loved ones in the Air Guard, and if they did had they heard the news?

At the sound of someone coming up from behind, she turned to greet Doctor Arne Morrison. His usual crooked smile was missing and there was even more of the usual intensity in his dark eyes as he walked toward her.

"I'm sorry, Jan. I just heard."

"I'm still trying to face up to it, but it's not going to be easy. Sorry, I'm not quite on top of everything this morning."

The doctor put his arms around her. "Cry on my shoulder if it will make you feel better," he said. "I had hoped those orders might not come through, after all. But I understand they did. I'm sorry."

Jan began to cry. "I knew it was coming," she said. "I thought I was ready for it, but I'm not. I'm sorry, Doctor Morrison."

"Don't be sorry for showing your emotions, if that's what you mean. I wish more people around here felt free to do that. It's a lot better for us all than keeping things bottled up inside. Go ahead and cry on the old doctor's shoulder. That might be the best medicine I offer anyone today."

Jan gave him a squeeze, then pulled back. She still had tears, but she smiled. "You always make me feel better. You know there's a doctor or two who'd try to get me kicked off the nursing staff for what I just did."

"I suppose. You get a barn full of jackasses there's always two or three that bray louder than the rest. Nobody pays any attention to them. So did I hear correctly that he's going to Afghanistan? How long is the assignment?"

"Eighteen months, probably. I think it's sure to be more than a year, anyway." She wiped at her eyes with a tissue. "Things are going to blow up over there, Doctor Morrison. And Phil is going to be right in the middle of it."

"I hope not, but I have to admit it worries me you may be right. Damn, it all seems so useless. You just have to wonder what the future of mankind could be if we didn't have wars all the time. I'm a doctor, Jan, and I've devoted most of my life to helping heal human beings with every physical problem you ever heard of. One little war can take more lives in an hour than I've helped save in a lifetime."

"But that doesn't take anything away from what you've done, doctor. There are a lot of people walking around right now that might not be here without your good medicine."

Doctor Morrison's usual smile returned. "I think you mean *great* medicine. That's what we practice here at Memorial Hospital, remember?"

"If you say so."

The doctor turned and did a quick hands-on examination of the still and silent patient while Jan went about her usual chores of checking and recording vital signs. Nothing had changed. She waited for the doctor to give any new directives.

"Well, speaking of helping patients," he said, "it gets more apparent every day we're not going to be able to help this one. I honestly don't know what keeps him alive, other than his stubborn will to live."

"Yes, but sometimes that can go a long way."

Doctor Morrison turned to go, then paused. "Look," he said softly, "my little sermon wasn't what you needed to hear. The odds are fantastic that your husband comes through this without a scratch. The toughest role is going to be yours. Are you getting geared up to be a single mom?"

"I won't be ready by any means, but we don't have any choice."

"If you ever need more crying time we'll find it. I may even join you before we're done. But I'm getting philosophical, and that's not what Memorial Hospital pays me for. I guess we'd better get on with our doctor and nurse stuff—we have great medicine to practice!"

"Onward and upward?"

"Keep on keepin' on!" As he left the room, he thrust an arm in the air and pumped it, fist closed, as if to signal a stamp of determination.

27 / I smell the rot

I JUST WALKED THROUGH Aunt Nell's garden. It was lush with delphinium, pink and purple and more beautiful than I remembered. She was there too, crying, and Uncle Dick was trying to console her. I couldn't tell for sure what was wrong, but I think her little alabaster statue of the Christ child had been broken. I wanted to help but she never answered when I asked if I could fix the little Christ child and if I did would it help me get to heaven when I die. I thought she just didn't hear me, but now I think I may not really have been there. It might have been a dream.

I wish it was real, and I wish I had fixed the Christ child and I could feel good about it and think it would help me get to heaven. I think I may die soon. But if I do I won't go to heaven. I'm not a good person.

This room is hot. The furnace is running too long or maybe they don't have a way to control it. We had to have a new furnace put in the house in Chicago before we sold it and moved down to the Shawnee. Marilyn thought that was a good idea because I love trees. When you get a new furnace you have to have inspections and there was an inspector I thought was very nice and he turned out to be from down in Indiana somewhere like me and we talked about the Cubs and Bucky and I were going to a Cubs game before whatever happened. But something here doesn't fit. I may be confused.

I remember now, the accident. And we were going to a Cubs game and that means it is summertime and they don't have the furnace on. I hate being mixed up this way. It's not like me. Grandmama read to me from her little book of Tennyson poems and she said I understood them because I was a very smart little boy. I thought I was smart, too, but maybe I was lying to myself and Grandmama, both.

I loved my grandmother and I should not have lied to her. I should not have lied to Marilyn. But if I was smart I wouldn't be in Vietnam. The smart guys didn't have to be here because they made up excuses or got phony doctor's letters or went to college and didn't end up over here. Chaplain Lewis says their consciences ought to bother them and we ought to be proud we are fighting for our country. I went to college, but that was after I left here.

I smell the rot through the window and I know it's the swamp and jungle and we have to slough through it waist-deep and hold our rifles over our heads and not let them get wet but it doesn't matter if we get wet. Greer had some kind of foot disease because of his feet getting wet all the time. He got killed, I think. Terry and me got wet feet lots of times, but nobody cared because wet feet don't hurt little kids.

Little kids can't go off and fight in wars rich old men start. Uncle Dick said rich old men start the wars poor young men have to go and fight. He wanted me to study and be an engineer or a businessman when I grew up and be rich and he said if I was rich I wouldn't have to fight the wars like he did. I don't think he was in Vietnam, though. He liked to fish on the Ohio River, I remember that for sure.

I'm trying to slow my brain down. I don't think it was hot in here, but I felt hot. They were doing something to me and maybe they fixed whatever made me feel hot. I'm a teacher. I should be more careful when I talk. They hauled bullets in and bodies out, but they also hauled us out alive and some other guy and I rode out on the same dustoff call and they had us in a field hospital right away. But I think this is a real hospital. I think if they take the bandages off my face I can see better, and the first thing I'll notice is whether there are guys in uniform.

I wish I could see out a window. I wonder if there are any sycamore trees here. I can always tell the sycamores, because they are mostly white and kind of ghostly looking when all the leaves are gone. I don't remember if Tennyson ever wrote a poem about sycamores.

There used to be a big sweetgum tree just outside my window. Terry and I tried to find ways to make things out of the gum balls and there were so many of them. We thought if we could make things to sell from the gum balls we could be rich. Uncle Dick said getting rich from selling things was a lot easier than having to work for it. He worked hard, and he never got rich. Aunt Nell gave him a hard time.

Terry was in love with my mother, and then with Geri. My mother was beautiful. I didn't think Geri was beautiful, but Terry did. We hid and watched Geri naked all the time and I would have been embarrassed if Grandmama found out. There were naked women in that village, too, and soldiers did awful things to them. I don't know if Terry was in the war because he moved to Ohio and I never saw him again. Greer got killed in the war.

I think Greer reminded me of Terry. He and I arrived as replacements assigned to the First Battalion on the same day and both ended up in Charlie Company in the same rifle squad. He was a Texan without the Texas brag and we got to be good friends pretty quick. He actually was born somewhere in the East—Rhode Island, I think— but his father worked for a big oil company and they sent him to Texas when Greer was about ten years old. He grew up in Houston.

I don't want to talk about Greer, though. And you really don't want to hear what a trip-wire grenade hidden on a jungle trail can do to a human body. And I don't want to say anything that makes it sound like I'm using Greer as an excuse for anything I did.

I don't want to think about this anymore. I don't have to. I won't.

I am amazed at myself, sometimes. I just managed to make my brain slow down. It is like I made it stop and back up and start over again. All the same information is still there but now I can put it in some order and not have it all jumbled and spilling out at random.

Marilyn says brains are complex organs. She is a physical therapist, and she works with muscle and tissue and all the joints by which our bodies are connected. But she says everything we do begins in our head: "Think how many little impulses it takes just to guide your fingers to pick up a single pebble on the beach!" This is how she explains to patients that she can help with the fingers but they have to get their brain working, themselves.

She would understand that my brain is not working all that well right now. Those little impulses she talks about apparently are going astray. I can't tell if my fingers work at all, much less well enough to pick up a pebble on the beach. I wish they hadn't always worked so well. Those human beings I killed in Vietnam might still be alive. My fingers put all those bullets in my rifle. I never told Marilyn everything.

I wish Annie would come. I wanted them not to tell Craig, but that might have been because I was afraid he wouldn't come. I know Marilyn is here. Bucky might be here but I know Nita isn't. My grandmother and Uncle Dick would come but I think they died and Geri and Sissy don't care enough to come. They are getting pretty old, though, and maybe they are not able. I'm old. When I get it all stretched out in my brain I realize some of what I thought is now was a long time ago.

The human senses are miraculous things. We ought to rely on them more. If something tastes bad, don't eat it. If it smells bad it might be dead. If we don't hear anything it probably means there is nothing there to hear. If we touch a thing and it is sharp it will cut us. If what we see is beautiful we should look at it more often. Ugly is easy to find, but there is beauty, too, if we take the time to look.

Marilyn says our brain is simply a big computer that takes in what our senses tell us and processes the information and helps us understand what it means. She says it has immense memory capacity just like a computer and calls up what our senses have told us before so we don't have to learn everything over again.

So, okay, I remember now that this is where the argument between Annie and her mother began. Annie said the brain's memory is too easily compromised by what is already there, and much of the time does not separate new sensations from the old. She said the eye sees what it takes to the seeing and that's why people are prejudiced and support ignorant political candidates and destroy the environment and all the other things that sooner or later will doom humanity. Marilyn laughed at her, even though I know she agrees with a lot of this, and they more or less kept at each other until they had a big argument over how Annie bought something she didn't need and could have spent the money more wisely and Annie said it was none of her mother's business how she spent her money and I know they both feel bad about it and are just too proud to give in.

I thought about trying to lighten things up with a witty verse on pride from Alexander Pope. He said pride was vain when somebody "had no poet and they died." I think I knew what that meant at one time, but I don't now. And I didn't say it anyway because I was afraid Marilyn would be irritated I was hiding behind the words of a poet again and Annie would complain that I was too wishy-washy and should take a position on the issue between them.

When I fall back on the words of poets, I don't think it's hiding behind them. Tennyson's poetry, especially, seems to speak to me directly—like he actually knew me and understood what was going on in my mind and wrote about it. When he talks about the throbbing war drums I could almost think he had just been having a beer with some guy who was in the war and actually had heard them. I know I hear them, night and day. The throbbing comes and goes in intensity, but it's always there. And there's that marriage of music and poetry again. Led Zeppelin's "Kashmir" is much like Tennyson's throbbing war drums. The music drives deeper and deeper into my head and I keep hoping for a junction, a point at which I know this could be either the beginning or the end or I find I have different directions to choose from and I have to decide. And then the question is, would I know which way to turn?

One of the funny things I remember learning in school when I was little is that if two people turned different directions and kept on walking they would have to go all the way around the earth before they'd meet again. The teacher didn't know how far it is around the earth, and got mad when someone said they couldn't keep walking because they would come to an ocean. I used to know how far it is around the earth but I don't remember now.

There is a screen-saver on my computer that has large bubbles floating freely, bouncing at random, controlled only by their confinement within the limits of the screen. This is the way my brain feels, like that computer screen, with things bouncing around at random.

Impressions from the accident and the war and bits of poetry and memories of Annie and Craig and things I've told Marilyn and Bucky and Nita and things they've told me all run uncontrolled through my brain. I want to keep all my memories but I don't want to have them all trying to rise to the surface at once.

I thought I had slowed down my brain's activity, but I was wrong again. I have no such control.

I used to go up and play in the huge hayloft of Uncle Dick's big barn. There were cats up there. I guess they lived there, and sometimes there were kittens. I loved the cute little kittens. Nita had a cat. I don't think he liked me. Nita said he was jealous, especially after he saw us doing things. He bit me once and Nita said don't let him do that but I couldn't stop him. I knew his name but I don't remember it now. Nita loved him like a human.

I think it was Greer who was killed in the war, but it might have been Terry. I still see him in my nightmares all the time. Everybody told me he was dead but I didn't believe it, or anyway didn't want to believe it. I would have had to believe it, actually, because he was torn to pieces by that grenade or whatever it was they had tied to that vine he tripped over. Even if a Huey had come in there they couldn't have saved him. Chaplain Lewis said a prayer over him but it didn't do any good. I don't know why they have chaplains in war. There's nothing they can do.

28 / *Sissy*

SISSY ARRIVED AT HER brother's bedside in Room 12 of the Memorial Hospital ICU in a wheelchair, pushed by a tall young man who looked as if he took pride in his role. She was frail and obviously tired, but she was joking with the young man pushing her as they came down the hall.

Marilyn heard them and met her at the door.

"We made it!" Sissy proclaimed. "You can credit my young chauffeur, here. Has anything changed?"

Marilyn stood aside to allow space for her to be wheeled into the room, and close beside the patient's bed. "I'm glad you're here, Sissy," she said. "I wish I had better news but, no, I'm afraid nothing has changed. Did you have a good trip?"

"Very nice trip. Marilyn, meet my friend, Blake. He picked me up at my front door, drove me over here, and delivered me safe and sound. I never could have made it without him."

Marilyn and Sissy's driver exchanged greetings. He was polite but somewhat reserved, clearly not comfortable in the ICU setting. He made arrangements with Sissy for a time to come back for her and set off to find lunch and do some shopping in town. Sissy assured him she was in no hurry.

"Seems like a nice young man," Marilyn said.

"Oh, he's a delight." Sissy inched her wheelchair closer to the side of the bed. "It's painful to see him like this," she said, this time referring to her brother. "I've been heartbroken ever since you called. After all he's been through. Are the kids here?"

"Annie is. We haven't heard from Craig yet. And you remember his friend, Bucky. He's here."

"I remember Bucky. I'll be happy to see the kids. It's been so long since I've seen either one. But how are you holding up under all this, Marilyn?"

"I don't know. I'm just numb. I've tried to accept the inevitable, but I really haven't. There's no way ever to be prepared for something like this."

"Of course not. Not when it happens like this."

Marilyn turned and gazed out the window. She could see the red and white medevac helicopter on its landing pad atop a nearby building. Had it been there all along? She couldn't remember seeing it before. But surely she had, and she recalled Bucky mentioning it, and Greg, the flight nurse, had visited here in the room. Of course she had seen it. Was her exhaustion beginning to take a toll on her mental acuity? But then she realized Sissy was asking her a question.

"I'm sorry," she said. "My mind was wondering. I didn't hear what you said."

"It wasn't important. I just asked if you remembered him in his uniform."

"Actually, I never saw him in his uniform. He was out of the Army when I met him, and he never would put it back on."

"That's a shame. He was so proud to wear it in the beginning. He wanted to be a soldier, like Uncle Dick."

"We were just talking—Bucky and I—about how Uncle Dick was his father figure. He never would have said so, but I think he was jealous of you and Geri because of your relationship with your father. He always felt cheated, and thought his father didn't really care for him like he did for you girls."

Sissy had turned her wheelchair so that she faced Marilyn. She sat silently for a moment, looking down and nervously fingering the handle of a small purse that lay on her lap. She raised her head and looked Marilyn intently in the eyes before she spoke.

"I'm not sure it's right for me to tell you this," she said. "Geri and I have kept it a secret all these years, and never wanted him to know. There were a couple of times we were tempted to tell him, thinking it somehow might make him feel better to know the truth. But I don't think it would have. We just found out by accident. Daddy came home drunk one night and he and our mom had a terrible quarrel that got so loud it woke us up. We heard her ask why he couldn't at least show a little affection for his son, like he did for us. And he said, 'Because I'm not as dumb as you think I am. I know the little shit's not mine.' She never answered."

"Good Lord. No wonder—"

"Maybe I shouldn't have told you. We don't even know if it's true. Our father wasn't much of a man, as it turned out. He moved off to New York City and pretty much abandoned us."

"He never mentioned his father. It was always Uncle Dick he talked about."

"I'm not surprised. His father gave him nothing to remember."

Jan came and began her periodic routine. The other two women stood aside and watched her work. When she had finished, Sissy introduced herself. Jan expressed her sympathy and added a note of gratitude that Marilyn had additional support.

"She stood watch pretty much all by herself for a good while," Jan said.

Sissy put a hand on Marilyn's. "He is lucky to have such a devoted and loyal partner," she said. "This woman has more patience and understanding than any other human I know. There have been a lot of times he might not have made it without her."

"I know she's happy to have you here."

After Jan left the room, the other two women—wife and sister, each with her own memories—sat and talked quietly about the past. One's story was a reminder to the other, and both learned a few new things about this man who lay like a corpse before them. Without realizing it, they slipped into speaking of him in past tense.

When Blake returned an hour later, Sissy was ready to go. She sat close to her brother's bed for a moment, with her hand on his shoulder, tears streaming down her face. "God be with you," she whispered, then turned back to Marilyn.

"I wish I had something positive to say," she said. "I don't see any chance he's going to make it. I would stay if I could, but I know you understand. Bless you, dear. I know you will keep me informed."

Marilyn grasped her hand, but didn't speak.

Blake told Marilyn goodbye and wished her luck. He carefully guided Sissy's wheelchair from the room and, once in the hallway, turned toward the elevators and pushed the chair more rapidly. Sissy lowered her head and sobbed softly.

Marilyn stood silently for a long while, studying the comatose man who lay before her as if seeing him for the first time. In her mind, she replayed the memories of days long past. The early days in Terre Haute came to the fore, recollections from that time when they were young and falling in love, each embracing the other's presence as a gift valued beyond measure.

She leaned in so that her face was close to his.

"Say over again, and yet once over again, That thou dost love me," she whispered. Her words were aimed at him, but spoken in softness such that they might have been meant only for herself.

"Remember, my sweet man? It's Elizabeth Barrett Browning. Those beautiful words you read to me so long ago, but words I've never forgotten. I kept that little book of sonnets, more precious to me now than ever before."

She was quiet again then, thinking back. This was the single person to whom she had given her life, offering her very being in unreserved devotion. She missed him now far more than she ever could have imagined.

She turned away from the bed and stepped to the window. The world outside had come alive as the day passed. Traffic on the streets below was heavy. Streams of people moved in all directions on the sidewalks. It was as if Memorial Hospital, at this instant, might have been the center of the universe. And for her, it was.

29 / *I may be confused*

I HOPE THEY'VE CALLED in the dustoff signal. I know I'm
hurt, bad. I think I may have lost an arm on one side
and I know I'm bleeding to death and the medics can't
save me out here in the jungle. I don't want to die here,
not in this putrid hell where the shooting and the killing
never end.

I wish I could see my grandmother and Uncle Dick
and I wish Terry would come around and we could go
down to the river and throw things in the water and
watch how fast they float away. When the Ohio River is
high the water is very swift. If I make it out of here I'll be
able to go home soon and see Grandmama. I don't think
Terry lives in Indiana any more.

I don't hear a chopper. I'm afraid they are not going
to get here in time. The big Hueys are loud, but sometimes you don't hear them till they are right on top of
you. I hope they've sent one.

When I was at Fort Leonard Wood they told us it
wasn't our job to die for our country, but to make somebody else die for his country. I think we made a lot of
people die today. Lieutenant Pinchuck would be proud
and probably would say his company trained me well,
except that all those people we made die were not soldiers. And Lieutenant Pinchuck would not want us to kill
innocent civilians.

I think I just had a birthday. I think I was twenty
years old. If you're going to be born you should have
longer than that on earth. That's what I think. Maybe
they should send old men to war instead of young men.
Uncle Dick was old, but he was young like me when he
was in war. I'm glad he wasn't killed.

I may be confused again. I don't think I'm in Vietnam anymore. If I am, I'm wounded and they'll have to get me out of here. I think I'm already in a hospital, though, and I can tell the bleeding's stopped. How much blood does an adult human body hold? There were so many of us who needed so much blood, I wonder how they didn't run out. I don't remember what type of blood I have. I used to know. It was important when I was in the war but I don't think it is now. The Vietnamese in that village didn't have blood for their wounded and it probably didn't matter. Most of them already were dead. I think the hearing officer asked me about that, if there were wounded people we tried to help. I don't remember his name but he was a captain.

It bothers me to be confused. Grandmama always said I was a smart little boy but I haven't seen her in a long time. She may not think I'm smart anymore.

I think I dreamed about Rosie Leck. I remember her from work. And I remember we discussed war. Not Uncle Dick's war nor mine, but the Civil War. Miss Leck was young and pretty and taught history and knew about the Civil War. I wanted to know about the Civil War because I was telling my students about Stephen Crane's book, *The Red Badge of Courage.* I've read it three or four times. I think he understood war very well for not having been in one. I used his work in class to show students what creative writing is all about—the ability to create reality in the imagination and tell the story in such a way readers believe you've actually experienced it. And how, while his story is about the Civil War, his characters might have been soldiers in any war.

One of the students, who knew I'd been in war, asked if *I* found Crane's characters real. I did. We got into a good discussion about war and how, no matter the differences among all the wars through history, every one of them led to many people suffering and dying. When you look back at a war, you need to ask whether it

had to be fought. I know the big war, World War II—
Uncle Dick's war—had to be fought so a madman like
Hitler couldn't take over the world. And the Japanese. I
forget about the Japanese because Uncle Dick didn't fight
them.

The student said the Civil War had to be fought to
end slavery, and I agreed. We thought of some other
wars but didn't know enough about them to decide. And,
anyway, I wanted to talk about literature and poetry and
not about war.

I read Stephen Crane's book the first time long after
I left Vietnam and I've always wondered if it would have
made much difference if I had read it before. I really
identified with his soldier beginning to envy a wounded
comrade and feeling like the wounded were better off. I
remember feeling the same way after no more than a
few weeks in Vietnam. A wound that did not kill you
might be a ticket home.

I changed my mind about that pretty fast when I
actually got shot, myself. Until you see it—or, worse, feel
it—you couldn't possibly believe the damage bullets from
a rifle made for war can do when they rip through flesh
and bone. My wounds got me home, but I would have
been glad to trade another year, or whatever time I had
left to serve, for the pain this ripped-up shoulder and
arm has caused me over the years.

Miss Leck knew a lot more about the Civil War than
she did about Vietnam. She said the reason so many Civil
War soldiers came home missing limbs simply was in-
fection. I said yeah, I guess their field hospitals weren't
very sanitary and she said yes but it was more often
because the bullet fired by the Civil War rifle—the mini
ball, just a little round ball of soft lead—was not high
velocity and flattened out when it smashed into the
target and dragged all kinds of dirt and cloth fragments
and whatever along with it into the soldier's arm or leg
or wherever it hit.

I don't know if this is true, but she seemed confident it was. And she was interested to hear about bullets in Vietnam.

I guess I made a fool of myself when she asked me about this, because I started out talking about my own wounds and then before I knew it I was talking about old women with babies in their arms and I broke up and started crying and Miss Leck was embarrassed and didn't know what to do and sorry she ever tried talking to me about war. I'm sorry, Miss Leck. I really am.

I told Bucky about all this sometime later. He said she should have known that I was in Vietnam and not even bought up the war. I didn't agree, but I always respected Bucky's opinion. He was there, too, as I may have made clear before, and spent a lot more time in battle than I did. That's why he understands me.

Bucky was a sad-looking excuse for a soldier the first time I saw him. The first thing you notice is his flaming red hair and his skin color, which is kind of pink. He is a short man, and by his own admission bow-legged, which means he looks funny when he walks. He was scare-crow skinny and with his severe wounds barely able to walk at all. I probably did not look like much, either, but I couldn't see myself so I didn't know. Maybe it was because we both were pretty much at the bottom of the barrel that we made a quick connection and have been like blood brothers ever since.

Given the length of time he spent wading around in the swamps and that endless jungle, I'm not surprised that Bucky got just about all the fevers and staph infections and the like that guys got over there. He just found out a year or so ago that he may have problems now from liver flukes he picked up way back then. His company was cut off from their battalion for weeks and ran out of rations and had to eat whatever they could get their hands on. You could get all kinds of parasites that way, and now they're saying that guys who ate uncooked or undercooked fish out of Vietnam rivers and streams were very likely to have picked up liver flukes.

Just the thought of liver flukes is repulsive. I don't want to think about them. I don't want to think about the war anymore.

I think I need to get some rest. I want to sleep and dream about heaven again and if I wake up I want to think about the future and not stress so much over the past. But I've done too many things wrong, and now I'm afraid I'll never have a chance to try to make up for that. How will anyone know I'm sorry if I don't live to tell them?

30 / Kendra

KENDRA'S FACE TOLD Jan there was a problem, and Jan rushed to her to find out what it was. "What's the matter?" she demanded, not bothering with empty preliminary greetings. "You look like you've got trouble on your mind this morning. What's going on?"

"It's worse than I thought."

"What's worse? Here, let's go over here to the family lounge where we can talk. There's nobody in there right now."

They moved across the hall and two doors down to the lounge, and Jan held the door for Kendra to enter ahead of her. Kendra took only a couple of steps into the room, then turned back to face her directly. It was apparent that she had been crying, her eyes red and slightly swollen, and Jan's concern surged to a higher level.

"We're in big trouble," Kendra said. "Mark hadn't told me everything. Jan, he owes a lot of money. More than we have. I don't know what we're going to do."

"Here. Let's sit down, and I'll get us some coffee and we can talk about it. Okay?"

She motioned toward a couch and chairs at the end of the room and Kendra took a seat on the couch and waited patiently while Jan went into the small kitchen and got coffee in throw-away cups. Jan struggled to compose herself, hoping to offer a calm demeanor before she began any discussion. Letting her own anxieties show was the last thing she wanted to do. She moved slowly, bringing the coffee and taking a seat in one of the chairs facing Kendra.

"Now, tell me what's going on," she said.

"Mark told me everything last night. He's lost a ton of money doing that gambling on the Internet, and we don't have enough to pay off his debts. I'm afraid we're going to lose everything, even our house. And now we've got the baby coming and everything and . . . . "

Kendra's voice faltered and she began to cry.

"I'm sure there's a way out of this," Jan told her. "Have you talked to anyone else about it? I mean, there have to be people who know about these things. You know I'll help any way I can."

"I don't think you can help. He owes too much, and he's going to get in big trouble if he doesn't pay. He thinks there may be gang money involved."

Jan didn't know what to say. Kendra needed advice desperately, but this was way over her head. She felt helpless, and at the same time angry with herself. She had encouraged Kendra to be open about her troubles and now that it was happening she could only sit like a fool and struggle for words. She scolded herself mentally. *It's put up or shut up time, Jan. So what are you going to do?*

But someone was at the door.

Jan stood and, walking behind Kendra, put a gentle hand on her shoulder as she hurried to the back of the room and answered the soft knocking. She opened the door and Marty stood in the hallway.

"Hey, guys, I don't want to intrude," she said loudly, "but you're wanted on the phone, Jan."

Jan turned back to Kendra and told her she would be gone for only a few minutes. Then she slipped out the door, and to her surprise Marty reached out and took her arm as if to keep her from walking away. Marty put a finger to her lips to signal silence, led her a few steps back from the door and stopped. Jan waited expectantly.

"Sorry for being weird about it," Marty whispered, "but I need to talk to you out here first."

"What's going on?"

"Mitch just called. He told me what's happening with Mark and Kendra. I'm guessing she's talking to you about it, and I didn't want to interrupt, but Mitch says there's new information she might need to know about."

"God, I hope it's good information."

"It is."

"Then let's go tell her."

Jan led the way back into the lounge. Kendra obviously was surprised by Marty's presence, but managed a wan smile and greeted her with a softly spoken, "Good morning."

"Hey, kid," Marty said. "I got something to tell you. Something important."

Kendra was hesitant, and looked at Jan as if seeking approval.

"It's good news," Jan said. "Marty, go ahead and tell her. She needs to hear this."

Marty raised a hand, palm facing outward, in a mock peace sign. "I'd be the last one on earth to poke into your business, Kendra," she said. "but 1 know what's happening and I've got information that will be good for you to hear. But, both of you, understand that this is highly confidential, though. Mitch could get in big trouble if they found out he'd let this out."

"Marty, if you're giving me some BS I'll kill you!" Kendra declared.

"It's not BS. This is real stuff. But you both have to swear on your grandmother's Bible not to breathe one word of this."

"Marty!" Jan's demanding tone reflected her frustration.

"Okay, okay. Here's the deal. Mitch's law firm has been working with a task force appointed by the attorney general's office to investigate illegal gambling in the state. You can understand why it's top secret. I don't know any more about it than what I'm about to tell you guys. But the bottom line is, Mark is among a whole lot of people suckered in by a crooked operation that did not make book through a licensed establishment like they claimed. They're going to be shut down."

"So what does this mean for Mark?" Kendra asked. "He lost a ton of money to these guys."

"That's why Mitch wanted me to tell you. He won't have to pay it. There's no way this phony operation will be allowed to collect. The state's going to be moving in on them any day now."

"Are you sure about all this, Marty? I need to let Mark know. He's desperate enough I'm afraid he could do something drastic."

"I know, kid. This is the reason Mitch took the risk of letting this information out. Just make sure Mark understands it's still totally hush-hush."

Kendra already was digging her phone out of her purse. Marty motioned to Jan that the two of them should leave. They slipped out quietly and hurried back to the nurses' station, leaving a greatly relieved Kendra privacy to call her husband.

Jan was eager to give Marty her due: "That took some guts! You just saved those guys a world of worry."

"Hey, it took nothing on my part. I just carried the message."

"But it was a risky message. You knew you were taking a chance, letting the word get out."

"Mitch would never have let it get out except that they are going to move in on those guys, like, today. And, anyway, like Kendra said, Mark could be getting pretty desperate. Sometimes you just have to do what you have to do."

"You are a good person, Marty."

Jan put a hand on Marty's shoulder and gave her a pat, then stepped closer and embraced her. She knew Marty was rationalizing her action, even if her explanation was true. Marty had taken a big chance out of real concern for Kendra.

Marty's revelation had lifted an immense burden of anxiety from Jan, too. She could strike Kendra's situation from her own list of worries. But now the hard truth. Paradoxically, her apprehension over Kendra's problem had masked to some extent her larger, personal unease over the coming activation of the Air Guard and the life-altering absence of Phil's companionship for months to come. She knew there would be no new information such as Marty had brought to Kendra that would rescue her from this looming challenge.

31 / *I did my duty*

I KNOW THAT, WHETHER it's fair or not, you go through life being judged by others. And I know that when you're in an infantry company rifle squad in a fire fight, nobody cares who you are or where you're from. They just want you to fill your link in the chain. You cover a zone with bullets and the zones overlap and you destroy every living thing hiding out there in the jungle and then you move forward and do it all over again.

And I suppose this is the way it should be. If I do my job and carry my fair share of the load, what difference does my name make or where I'm from or what my mother fed me for breakfast or if my daddy really is a state trooper? A rifle squad is a good example of how effective a cooperative endeavor can be when everybody does their job. We did our job so well we didn't leave many pieces for someone else to pick up.

What it comes down to, I guess, is the fact that I would have taken some pride in my performance if our job had been something positive. I've been trying all these years to find something positive in killing people and I still have not been able to.

Why can't the effort put into killing be aimed at something good? There is a lot of good in the world, a lot of beauty. In my mind's eye I see images of children in that village that day and images of Craig and Annie and I know that all children are beautiful. How could we ever justify killing children?

I want a chance to talk to Bucky again about the war. We both know the sights and the sounds and smells of a fire fight and the sheer terror of being dropped by a Huey into an open patch in the jungle, hoping the door gunners with their M-60s killed every living thing when they sprayed the area with bullets but knowing they didn't, knowing you probably have an enemy rifle aimed at your heart even before you have both feet on the ground.

We both know the hopelessness and the pain of holding a buddy in your arms when the medics didn't get to him in time to stop the bleeding and you feel his life ebbing away and you want to go out and kill somebody for revenge and maybe it doesn't matter who. I know that even though the war was a long time ago it never will go away and the shooting goes on and on and some nights you don't want to go to sleep because you can't stand another nightmare.

I know it was more than our common experience in the war that brought Bucky and me together. Each of us needed a friend, and found one. We liked each other and enjoyed each other's company from the get-go. But it was the same path that led us to a common place at a common time, and that path was the war.

Like me, Bucky joined the Army as an escape. His life was headed nowhere and he was going to be drafted, anyway. The Army recruiters had a way of making military life look pretty exciting. You got a uniform and everything else you needed and you got to go to exciting places and do exciting things and everyone would look up to you for serving your country and you would come home a hero. This is what they told us.

They did not emphasize the point that serving your country might mean killing people, but to the extent this was understood you were led to believe the people you'd kill would be people who deserved it. They were a menace and yours was a call to help protect the world from their dangerous advance. Someone else already had decided this; you didn't question their decision.

Bucky believed this, just as I did. Whether believing was a convenient rationalization that let us use the Army as an escape was a question we chose not to confront. We had found what we were looking for.

Looking back now, Bucky as he was when we first met is the way I like to remember him. He tried not to look at the world as a bad place, and helped me see past the ugliness and hope for something better in the future. For Bucky, unfortunately. this better world centered on Nita. She was the best thing that ever happened to him and the worst. I wish there never had been a Nita.

We were going to go to a couple of Cubs games when I got to Chicago. Maybe it's just as well I didn't make it. We would have had a few beers and got melancholy about the war and got all hung up on the past and I might have broken down and told him. I hope he would have just beat the hell out of me, because I deserve it and would have felt better. But that wouldn't have happened. I'm sorry, Bucky.

I wish I could hear Annie's voice. I think I may never see her face again, but maybe I'm just getting discouraged. It has been too long.

Annie always is a happy memory. She would have been a joy to any father. She was a curious child, interested in the world around her and eager to learn new things. She asked me lots of questions. Marilyn said it was as much about getting Daddy's time as it was real curiosity, but I never believed that. Annie wanted to know how things worked and what made things happen.

There probably never was a parent who didn't look back once their children were grown up and gone and wish they had done things better. Uncle Dick used to say people should be like birds: feed their babies and protect them until they got out of the nest and learned to fly, then let them go their own way and never look back. I think now this may have been an excuse for his failure with his own kids. He was a fascinating story teller, though, and when I was little I thought everything he said was true.

I don't believe I told you about his children. He never talked about them. I think he had two sons and had a falling out with them and finally they just didn't have any contact anymore. My mother told me this, but she didn't know much about it. I won't be judgmental. I have failed too often in life to even pretend to judge anyone else.

Marilyn has been a rock, but she deserved better than me. She and I are much different in temperament.

Not really fire and ice, but I would be a poet and she would be a scientist or mathematician. That's the only way I can think to describe it. She doesn't get worked up emotionally the way I do. She wants things to be orderly and she doesn't like surprises. I've always admired the way she can draw analogies to explain things and make them seem more simple.

Just an example: No one else I know could reduce the complex emotional experience of sex to a formula like she does. She says in "proper" sex, even if the act itself is brief, the pleasure lasts for a long time in the form of emotional satisfaction. In "improper" sex, the pleasure ends as soon as the act is finished because the emotional satisfaction is replaced by regret. Conscience, again.

I never asked her to define proper and improper sex. I didn't need to.

It didn't happen often, but there were times when students came to me with problems involving sex. I wasn't supposed to deal with things like this. The school district's rules said I should send them to a school counselor. Marilyn insisted I should follow the school's rules, primarily because counselors were trained to handle this and I wasn't. And she said if I tried to work with the student, myself, I was assuming responsibility for the outcome and if things didn't go well I could be blamed for the consequences.

Her view certainly was the wiser one—the mathematician's way of seeing things, I suppose. But I was the would-be poet and I couldn't help but see the pain in some boy's or girl's eyes and want to help take it away on the spot. I think I did help a couple of times, and I don't believe I ever made things worse. I could have, though, and I was wrong to deal with the issue the way I did.

And no student would come to me for advice today. Not if they knew the things I have done.

I will be honest. This could be a deathbed confession, so why wouldn't I be? I succumbed to temptation because Nita aroused me in ways I never thought possible. I wanted her from the very first time I saw her. I don't mean this in a vulgar way. She was beautiful and desirable and I felt a chemistry between us. And this was a two-way street, if you know what I mean. She felt the chemistry, too, and anytime we were in the same place at the same time it was almost as if there was a magnetic force pulling us closer. Had we both been single, I have no doubt we would have made love the first night we came in contact.

And the attraction was a personal thing, not some lurid desire for the unattainable. What I mean is, I wasn't on the make, just looking for a fling. I was not attracted to "other" women. I was attracted only to Nita. She gave every sign of feeling the same about me.

It would have been easy enough to deal with this situation if I had seen Nita only occasionally, but because Bucky and I were as close as brothers it was a lot harder. There rarely was a week the four of us—Bucky and Nita and Marilyn and I—weren't together three or four times. We visited in each others' homes, went out together to eat, went to movies together, checked in to see what was going on in the other household nearly every day or night. I recognized the danger of Nita's constant presence, but I did nothing to head off the inevitable. And my brotherly love for Bucky was my excuse.

I was weak. There never was a time when Marilyn was not a good wife. The passion never left our relationship. I could have and should have been satisfied in my marriage. Temptations are a fact of life. As Matthew Henry wrote, though, many a temptation "comes to us in fine gay colors that are but skin deep." I should not have succumbed so easily. But I did.

There are no lurid details. I went by their house one day after work to return a CD I'd borrowed and no one answered when I rang the bell but the door was not locked and I went in. The living room was empty. I walked back toward the family room to put the disk on a rack Bucky kept there, and as I started down the hall Nita stepped out of the bathroom naked. She had been in the shower and not heard me at the door. When she saw me she froze in place and blushed almost a deep purple, but she made no move to cover her body. She opened her arms as I walked toward her.

There is nothing more to tell. We went into the bedroom—hers and Bucky's—and made love. We knew it was wrong. We did it because, at that instant, we wanted each other so much nothing else mattered.

I wish I could tell you this was the only time, that we were caught up in circumstances we didn't intend and never let it happen again. But in truth, we relished our illicit affair like two randy teenagers who had just discovered the pleasure of sex and had no moderating influence to sway us from playing the game. Over the next several months, planning the secret rendezvous became our routine.

It was a combination of guilt and desire that led me to just lose it one night when we were all together. I broke up and lost control and got so emotional Marilyn and Nita were worried and took me to the emergency room. And then, three days later, suddenly and without warning, Nita packed a small bag, told Bucky she was going to visit her sister in Miami, and never came back.

Bucky was at our house almost every night for the next three or four months, drinking vodka martinis and crying on Marilyn's shoulder and saying how life without Nita was too much to bear. He and I slipped into talk about the war more than once, and it was on one of these occasions that he said if he had the courage he'd just go stand in front of a train and end it all.

Given what I knew of Bucky's strength, it should not have surprised me that one night he showed up with a new attitude. But it did. A different Bucky from the one who had been there the night before stood in the kitchen and told us matter-of-factly that he still had a life to live and Nita was a thing of the past. I don't think I ever heard him mention her again.

I hear the music now. It's not loud enough. I can't tell what it is. Eerily beautiful instrumental. Might be one of my favorite rock bands, the Who. Roger Daltrey and Pete Townshend. No, there are familiar lyrics. It is the Moody Blues, "Nights in White Satin." Poetic but haunting, repetitive, never this and never that. Forbidden love. The words might have been written about my feelings for Nita.

Love should always be better than war, but love can be destructive, too. I had no right to do what I did. What I did in secret I would be deeply ashamed to have exposed and open to view. I wronged Marilyn deeply and I wronged Bucky, and these are the two people I love most. I cannot claim to be an honorable man.

32 / *Marilyn and Margie*

MARILYN RAN TO MEET her sister. Margie threw open her arms and the two women stood together in a long, tight embrace before either spoke. When they separated, both had tears in their eyes.

"I'm sorry I couldn't get here sooner," Margie said, as they walked into Room 12. "How are you doing?"

"I'm just glad you are here now. I've really needed you."

"I know it's tough. Are you holding up okay?"

Marilyn looked away for a moment, as if she needed time to consider her response. She turned back to face Margie, but still was slow to answer. "I'm just existing," she said. "I'm just going through the motions, I guess. It is kind of like, I don't know, nothing is real or something. I thought I had accepted it, but deep down I keep getting this feeling that it's not happening, that I'll wake up in the morning and find out it was all a bad dream. Then reality sets back in."

"Oh, honey, I know. Nobody should ever have to go through this. Are the kids here?"

"Annie is. Craig hasn't made it yet, but I'm sure he's on his way. And Bucky's here."

Margie stepped close to the bed in the middle of the room for the first time and looked down at the motionless occupant. "He's such a sweet man," she said. "He's always been a poet at heart, and I know he must have been a wonderful teacher. Has anything changed since I talked to you?"

"No. It isn't going to change. We're just waiting for the end."

Margie lowered her head and began to cry. She stood a while longer, tears streaming down her face, before turning back to Marilyn and stepping toward the chair under the window. She sat down and put her purse on the floor at her feet and Marilyn came and sat beside her.

"I hate so much to see him like this," Margie said, "and I hate to see you having to go through it and there's nothing I can do to help."

"Maybe that's some of what I'm feeling. My whole life, you've always had my back. I always felt safe when we were kids because my big sister was there to take care of me. You wouldn't believe how much I came to depend on you. And now you're here and I have to accept the fact that things are not the same and this time there is nothing you can do."

"I'm so, so sorry. We all love him. You know that. Daddy was as happy as I ever saw him when you told us you two were getting married. And I soon went from thinking he couldn't be good enough for my little sister to knowing he was the best. Daddy bragged about his great son-in-law to anyone who would listen."

Marilyn managed a smile. "He loved Daddy, too. I think he mourned his passing even more than we did."

Margie's spirits visibly brightened as the two reminisced. They exchanged stories about the man who lay silently before them in the middle of the room, each story flowing with feelings of deep affection. Margie told how he pretended to like country music because it was their father's favorite, which Marilyn knew but had forgotten. Marilyn talked about a time the two men saw a double rainbow and grew philosophical about the deep meaning of life

"We weren't allowed to see it often," she said, "but Daddy really was a deep thinker and he brought it out."

"Working men usually didn't talk that way among themselves. We knew Daddy was really smart, but he always said he was not an educated man. He said high school was as far as he wanted to go because he found school boring and all he wanted to do was get a job and go to work."

"Do you remember the double rainbow?"

"Now that you mention it, yes. They agreed that it represented something about life and life was 'incomprehensible.' That's what they said." She began to laugh. "Then they had a long discussion about exactly what that word meant. I remember being fascinated by their conversation. I didn't follow it, but it seemed profound even though it was down-to-earth. I felt like I was sitting at the feet of Plato or Aristotle or such. Thank you for bringing that up."

"Yeah, it was always fun when they got together. I'm just surprised he didn't teach Daddy to love Tennyson!"

Margie moved back to the bedside and stood over the patient again. This time there was something of a smile on her face. She stayed there for only a moment, then told Marilyn she was hungry and would like to go find somewhere to eat.

"You probably need to go, too," she said. "Come and tell me where to go and I'll buy you lunch. I have a rental car in the garage."

Marilyn said she had planned to stay in the room and wait for Bucky and Annie, but quickly decided there was no need for that and agreed to go. She didn't tell her sister, but she also was hungry, having skipped breakfast as usual. Besides, she was enjoying the time with Margie very much and didn't want it interrupted.

They drove to a restaurant Marilyn had discovered near her motel and liked. They found it crowded and went a block farther to a fast food drive-through, got cheeseburgers and French fries and drinks, and parked in a shady area and ate in the car. This turned into a fun event, calling up memories of their teenaged years together in Indianapolis.

"When this is all over, I want you to come to Philadelphia and spend a few weeks with me," Margie said. "We have missed too much because of the miles between us."

Marilyn agreed. "I will," she said. "And I want you to come and visit us—I'm sorry, come to visit me. I wish you could have come before. He would have loved to have you down in the Shawnee, with so much to show you."

"You call it that from the Indians, right?"

"Yes. It was all Indian country."

"You might say you're living in the shadow of the Shawnee."

"That sounds like the title for a book. Did you just make that up?"

"Of course," Margie said. "I can be very creative, you know. So, were the Shawnee peaceful?"

"Tecumseh was Shawnee."

"Meaning?"

"He was the great warrior who organized the tribes and led fierce war against the white settlers."

"Got it. You should have been my eighth grade history teacher."

Their lunch finished now, it was time to choose their course for the next few hours. They would return to Memorial Hospital and sit again in Room 12 of the Wing C ICU. The patient there was their center of interest, and would be until something changed.

Change would come. This was something they need not speak more of. He would not recover. They would sit by the window and talk, stand over him and speak to him, saying what they knew were empty words, perhaps shed more tears. He would not hear their voices. They would not see the love in his eyes. They would maintain that watch until well into the night and expect to return tomorrow to repeat the vigil, still without hope but with growing acceptance.

33 / *I did the white room*

I LOOKED INTO HER green eyes and it was like looking into a whirlpool and trying to see to the bottom. There was no bottom. These eyes could draw you in and take control of your mind and body. If I'd been a young man and this a romantic encounter, I would have fallen in love with this woman on the spot. But I wasn't so young and it was not a romantic encounter. I was in the white room and she was the psychiatrist on call.

She leaned in, close to my face, and demanded that I look her squarely in the eyes and give her my word that I would do nothing to harm myself. And I felt her total commitment to me, her alarm, her concern for my well-being, her fear that I actually might take my own life. I wish I could see her again and tell her these things mattered. I entered that room feeling my life was worthless, but I walked out believing this young doctor did care. And I might tell her she had beautiful eyes.

I know. Not everyone understands what I mean by "white room." I've heard it as a term for skiers—you get surrounded by walls of snow—and people try to make different things out of the lyrics of Cream's recording of a song by that name. I mean it the way people in medicine talk about it. It's the room where they put you on suicide watch. A sterile room. Nothing there you can use to finish yourself off.

Marilyn and Nita took me to the emergency room that night because they were afraid I was losing control. I could not stop crying. I had looked at myself in the bathroom mirror and told myself the world would be a better place without me. I still believe that, but generally I am not inclined to bring about such an end. And just now it seems hypocritical even to make this claim because I am determined to cling to life with one last hope of making amends. That night I had given up.

Bucky and Nita had come to our house for dinner and we were supposed to be celebrating something—I don't remember what. Bucky had had too much to drink and began to rehash the war and talk about the endless pain in his limbs and how he had so little to hold on to except me and how every night he said a little prayer giving his thanks that I was his best friend and always there for him and his confidence that, come hell or high water, I would never let him down..

Marilyn had been playing Elton John, Nita's favorite, on the stereo, and then put on an Eagles music video because Bucky loved the Eagles band and she wanted to cheer him up. The next I knew they were doing "Lyin' Eyes."

I tried not to look at Nita. But I did. Her face was frozen, expressionless. There was enough hurt in her eyes to melt the coldest heart that ever beat with life. She caught my glance and looked away.

I could have said for Nita all the things she wanted to say, the words, too difficult, that would have caught in her throat, words that could have been aimed at me but stalled by her own conscience because she was guilty, too. And I think it bothered her a lot that the first time something actually happened, she was the one who made the first move and let us slip past that bitter point of no return.

Marilyn, sitting next to Bucky on the ratty old sofa that dominated our living room, put her arm around him and pulled him to her side, his head resting on her shoulder. Bucky tried to say more, but the alcohol took over and he went to sleep. A little while later I helped Bucky to a bedroom, where mercifully he passed out. Marilyn went to the kitchen and made sandwiches. Nita and I sat and looked at one another, neither of us saying a word.

When I couldn't stand it any longer I went to the kitchen and pretended to help my wife for a few minutes and then went to the bathroom. One glance in the mirror and I felt all the self-hatred I'd been holding back and it just started spilling out.

I was a man who deserved no mercy. How could I go on sharing my bed with Marilyn and my home with Bucky as if nothing had happened? Could I go on with the great pretence that I had done no wrong? The bloody bodies of old women and the babies in their arms haunted my nightmares, but Marilyn and Bucky helped fill the hours and days of my life. There was no space between us. How could I even let them breathe the same air, much less speak to me of love and friendship and trust and loyalty? Fidelity is more than just a word.

I wanted to scream to the world what a despicable human being I was, how I had hurt those I love who loved me back, how I had shot the bullets that splintered the bodies of people who weren't shooting at me. I wanted to confess to Marilyn and Bucky and hope, even if I did not believe, there was a God in heaven who would magnify my declaration of guilt and echo it into some forsaken village in Vietnam. I wanted to, but I couldn't.

The doctor with the beautiful green eyes might have understood, but there was no occasion for me to tell her. The white room was not a place for counseling, not a place to lay out your tale of woe and hope to find sympathy and be told you are not a bad person. It was an integral unit of the emergency room and she was an emergency room doctor. Her job was to save me from myself, to bring at least a temporary end to such self-destructive tendencies as might be at work. She did, and I am grateful.

34 / *Jan and Doctor Morrison*

JAN STOOD CLOSE BESIDE the bed and studied the patient in Room 12. She had completed her routine and looked upon him not as a nurse responsible for his medical care, but rather as she imagined Marilyn would. How difficult it must be to await the inevitable end of his life this way, unable to communicate with him in any fashion and knowing he probably was unaware of her presence.

Surely Marilyn's heart was breaking. She put on a brave face, and Jan admired her courage. But there must be a point at which the weight became too heavy, a breaking point beyond the endurance of even one as strong as Marilyn.

She had come to avoid any effort to put herself in Marilyn's place, though, because even the merest idea that this could be Phil was too painful. What had been barely acceptable before was unbearable now that Phil was about to be sent into harm's way on the far side of the world in a land as foreign to her as the red planet Mars. She found little consolation in the fact that there was no ongoing war there at present. He would be in a danger zone where life was cheap and there were threats on every front.

Absorbed in her own thoughts, Jan was not aware that Annie had come up behind her. She was startled when Annie spoke.

"It's hard to see him this way."

"I'm sorry, I didn't hear you come in."

"You take care of patients like Daddy every day, I guess," Annie said. "Does it ever get to you? I mean, it must be hard to witness people dying day in and day out. I'm afraid I'd be depressed as hell."

"But it's not as bad as you think. Most of our patients live, and it is rewarding to see them pull through. I'm truly amazed sometimes at what the human body can be put through and survive."

"I'm glad then. I'm grateful for what you do."

Jan stepped back, to give Annie room close to the patient. "How's your mother doing?" she asked. "This has been an ordeal for her, as I'm sure you know."

"Yes, Mom's tough. But she's worn out. I'm trying to get her to spend less time here. I think she knows the end could come at any time and she wants to be by his side when it does. I guess we can't blame her for that."

"Have you heard from your brother?"

"No. We won't hear anything in advance. He'll just pop in. But I'm sure he's on his way and he should be here any time now."

Jan moved to the other side of the bed to adjust a bracket from which a plastic bag drizzled a thin stream of anticoagulant through a tube and needle into a vein in the patient's arm. She checked the remaining contents carefully, taking a quick measure of the remaining fluid.

"He's had enough of this," she said to Annie. "I'll take this one out of the way in a minute."

"I don't know how you know all you have to know. Anything to do with the practice of medicine has always seemed daunting to me."

Jan smiled. "I'm a nurse," she said. "It's easy for me. All I have to do is follow doctor's orders."

She stayed a while longer, pretending to wait to remove the fluid bag. But she wanted to visit more with Annie. Although she was not aware of this, she was beginning to feel as if Marilyn's family was her family, too. Annie could have been a model for the woman she wanted Emmie to grow up to be. In any case, she was not eager to get back to the nurses' station; a stack of paperwork would be waiting for her there.

A few minutes later, Jan had removed the fluid bag and was standing at the bedside computer when Doctor Arne Morrison arrived. He spoke briefly with Annie, then addressed Jan directly: "They told me I'd find you here."

"Were you looking for me, doctor?"

"Yes."

"Am I in trouble or something?"

"You may be, but not with me. I just wanted to visit with you briefly if you have a minute. If this young woman will excuse us, could we perhaps go talk in the family lounge?"

Annie said, "Of course," and stepped aside to clear the way.

The doctor walked at a rapid pace so that Jan had to hurry to keep up. Once inside the lounge, he turned back to face her. "I have something for you," he said.

"What is it?"

"This."

He held something toward her in a closed hand, waiting for her to reach out and take it. She offered an open palm and he dropped a heavy coin into it. She saw that it was a silver dollar.

"This is for Phil," Doctor Morrison told her. "Please give it to him and tell him I sent it for good luck."

"I don't know what to say," she said. "It's very thoughtful of you, and means a lot to me. Thank you!"

"It's been carried by men in the Morrison family through three wars, World Wars one and two and Vietnam. Everyone who carried it came through without a scratch. I hope it brings that same good luck to your husband."

Jan's eyes filled with tears. "You are such a sweet man, Doctor Morrison," she said. "I don't know how I can ever repay you."

He took her empty hand in his and squeezed. She saw that his eyes were misty, too. "Just bring him home safe and sound," he said. "And don't tell anybody. I've got to protect my grumpy old man reputation."

They went back to Room 12, where Annie sat quietly in the wide chair against the wall beneath the window. She looked up when they entered and smiled, but said nothing. Jan assessed and recorded the patient's vital signs while the doctor inspected the various casts and wrappings encasing his limbs. He found nothing new or different.

35 / I hate the world

IHAVE TO QUESTION Tennyson's contention that no life
"that breathes with human breath" has ever truly
longed for death. Lord Tennyson may have survived
some difficult family relationships, but he never set foot
on a battlefield and was not in a wreck on an interstate
highway. He suffered no long term illness, nor even the
normal ravages of old age, and lived a sheltered life of
ease and privilege. It wouldn't have occurred to him that
there often comes a point where life no longer is worth
living and death might look like an easy way out.

I suppose much depends on how you look at death to
begin with. If you believe in eternal life, why would you
not welcome death as merely the beginning of a new
adventure? An ancient prayer I read somewhere says
death is only a horizon and a horizon is only the limit of
our sight.

My journey has been long. I've seen my share of the
beautiful and the ugly and known my portion of the evil
and the good. I've had the exquisite thrill of watching
Marilyn give birth to a daughter and a son, felt the
warmth of a grandmother's lap and come to love the
serenity of a grandmother's voice, reading the poems
from her little book of Tennyson. I know the gratitude
on the face of an uncertain student who discovered the
beauty of poetry and I count myself richly rewarded by
having a friend like Bucky.

I've witnessed the splendor of the flowering redbud
and dogwood trees on a wooded hillside in the spring
and the glorious color of the white oak and sweetgum in
the autumn. I've found simple pleasure in the sparkle of
calm waters flowing down the Ohio River on the way to

their marriage with the mighty Mississippi and continued journey to the sea.

Ugly images surface easily, too: streams of children's blood in a remote village in a distant land, the waist-deep muck of a jungle that served as launch point for warriors bent on shooting and killing, the napalm fire rained down by screaming jet airplanes and the animals and human beings it roasted to little piles of carbon or eternalized in wretched, grotesque posture like statues carved by Satan's angels. I've felt the devastating impact of bullets from a military assault rifle ripping through my body and the crushing force of vehicles smashed into piles of scrap on a busy interstate highway.

And I've heard music. The music never deserts and never betrays. My body may be broken and useless, imprisoned in a solitary confinement, but my mind never fails to connect with the music. I hear the guitars and feel the guitars and always the drumbeat, driving, throbbing through my brain, and the brass, the violins. There are times when I wish the music would go away, times when there is too much music, times I wish the guitars would stop and the drumbeat cease and give my tired mind rest from the chore of identifying bands and separating what is real and now from what is merely residue from experience past.

But I need the music. Without it, how will I know if I'm still alive?

It's as if the music—slender thread though it may be—is my only connection to the real world I once inhabited. The music is of a place where there are people drinking coffee and telling family stories, a place of food and shelter with roofs that don't leak and painted walls of muted colors and windows with shades that open and let in the sunlight and lights over my head that conquer darkness, and a place where mothers put their children to bed at night without fear or worry because they have not been touched by war.

And there also was the other world, that world in which we killed innocent civilians and hopeless young men who probably didn't know why they were at war any more than I did. The soldiers. Bucky hated killing "gooks." He hated calling other human beings names like that and knew we called them that to make them seem different, less human, easier to kill.

Our squad leader pretended to be excited about getting into action and tried to get us all charged up to go out and kill some gooks. Killing is the only purpose an infantry company rifle squad has. That's what they gave us those M-16s for, he said. That's why they trained us to use them. We were the best the Army had—an outstanding killing machine.

"This weapon has only one use," he screamed, "and that is to kill! Today we're going to get the gooks who set traps that killed Greer and Granger. Think about those bloody bags of flesh and bone that used to be your buddies. Remember Greer and Grainger. Now get your sorry asses in gear and let's go! Kill, kill, kill!"

Oh, yeah. My nightmares are mostly about killing gooks. Baby gooks. I doubt they set any trap. But somebody set the one that killed Greer. Maybe I should try to remember this more often and not feel as guilty as I do for killing back. But I have tried, and it doesn't work. Hemingway said the world kills the good and the gentle and the brave and maybe he was right. But I hate the world for using me as an instrument for the killing.

I'm not afraid of hell, if there really is one. I live in it already, in the nightmares I still have about the war and in the pangs of guilt from which there is no escape no matter how deep I've tried to bury everything in my subconscious mind. I have killed other human beings and I have hurt the people I love who love me back.

The music, again. It can't be only in my head this time. It is too loud and too clear. The Rolling Stones, "Paint it, Black." I understand. I know it is said this song is not about war, but we thought it was and that perception became our reality. In a world at war, everything should be black. War doesn't go away. Night, day, night, day, there is no escape. War is a black world.

But their little village may have been flooded by sunshine that morning, a quiet, peaceful place until we came. Mothers fed their babies and children played on the floor. Did they hear the chop-chopping whirr of the blades on the big Hueys approaching and know they were war machines that would spew forth a devastating force of American soldiers? Did they feel the terror of knowing that a U. S. Army infantry company was about to obliterate life as they knew it? Did they have time to say they loved someone or clasp someone to them, body against body, before they were slaughtered in the name of saving the world from something they knew nothing about?

Uncle Dick was in the Battle of the Bulge and fought under General Patton. I guess he saw plenty of fighting, probably more than me, but their battles always ended sooner or later. Ours never did. He always said he was not a hero. He said he just did what he had to do. And he said there were things nobody knew about, like how they had some German prisoners and the captain had two guards walk them off into the woods and then the guards came back all by themselves. He said nobody asked what happened and nobody ever talked about it.

But just not talking about it doesn't make something go away. It hurt all the Vietnam guys to be called baby killers, and it should have. They did not kill babies. Not intentionally. But some soldiers wearing the same uniform did. I was there.

I want you to understand something, though. We didn't set out to kill those babies and those poor old men and women. The shooting just never stopped. If you haven't seen it you can't begin to understand how many bullets an infantry company can fire in only a couple of minutes. And then that goes on for hours, sometimes all day and all night. And they never let us run out of bullets. I would never have believed there could be that many bullets in the whole world. I can see in my mind's eye what bullets do to a baby but I can't talk about it.

I wish I had died in the war, early, before I killed other human beings. The anger I felt after holding the mortal remains of Greer in my arms was justified, but killing another person did not bring him back. Vietcong soldiers would have killed me if given that chance. They had their orders just like I had mine. But when we saw their bodies they always looked like kids. This was long ago, and maybe they could have had many good years ahead if they'd had the chance. They would be fathers and grandfathers now. What right did I have to end their life, any more than they had to end mine?

But the other thing wasn't so long ago. What I did to Bucky. And to Marilyn. And in a way, even, to Nita.

The other thing is not graphically vivid in my mind, like the war. The other thing is more on the outside, guilt for taking something that wasn't mine and I had no right to. It left images, too, but they are beautiful ones, pleasures of the flesh. I have no right to them, either, but sometimes they slip in and almost before I realize what I'm thinking I get old feelings I shouldn't have any more. Feelings about Nita. And then for a while these won't go away. Maybe I don't want them to. Now I remember the words of Dryden. He said pleasure after pain is sweet, and I can't help but think I've had my share of pain. But this pleasure was wrong. I don't deserve forgiveness.

If it falls my lot to talk one more time with Bucky, will I tell him? If I do, will it only hurt him more? How can I expect him to understand? I was supposed to be his best friend. He trusted me. I didn't mean to hurt Bucky.

I didn't mean to hurt Marilyn. Bucky is my friend, but Marilyn is my wife—the woman who gave me my due portion of happiness, who has been a wonderful mother to my children, who protected me against the world like the grandmother in the village that day holding her little child. Marilyn gave me the best of everything she had and I didn't mean to hurt Marilyn and I didn't mean to hurt Bucky and I didn't mean to kill grandmothers with their arms around the little children. But I did. I hurt them all.

There are beautiful natural areas in southern Illinois where we live now, forested hills interspersed with river valleys and floodplains and wetlands. And the stunning Garden of the Gods, with stone peaks and cliffs of monumental scale for a region without true mountains. I love it all with the poet's eye—the splendor I see before me—while Marilyn is fascinated by the natural history. She read that the geological strata in the Garden of the Gods is measured in time zones of millions of years, and there is a topographically important volcano that died before it reached the earth's fragile crust and came to life, but not before adding exotic minerals barely known except to the miners who dig the region's coal and fluorspar. She tells me of the salt mines and the ancient seas revealed through tiny fossils in the gravel dug from deep pits, and in her mind all these represent the natural order as it should be.

Her peace comes from natural order and mine from natural beauty. Uncle Dick's trees in the forest and fishes in the sea.

I would be quicker to give God credit for creating all this, and the mighty Ohio and Mississippi rivers that bound it, than I would for creating the likes of me. We live in a wonder world of nature's abundance and, for me, religion comes closer to explaining its origins than Marilyn's science does. Religion says it was *created*, while science flounders in trying to detail its beginnings.

I want to believe in God's creation and I want to believe in Chaplain Lewis' heaven. I want to believe that Grandmama is waiting there, hoping I show up with the little book of Tennyson poems and ready to sit and read through all eternity. I want to believe my mother is there, and Uncle Dick, and Terry and Greer and Granger. And if they are, then the grandmothers and babies from that remote village in the war and all the soldiers on both sides should be there, too, and the soldiers Stephen Crane wrote about, and Hemingway, and Ernie Pyle. Is there space, even in a universe of the vast dimensions known to science, for a heaven such as this?

And if there is, how can I believe I would be admitted? Is heaven not reserved for those who earned it? Or should I heed the words of Shakespeare, that "in the course of justice" *none* should see salvation, but hope for mercy as attributed to God?

I sense that my time may be running out. I can't tell. There isn't enough left of me to feel any difference. I'm scared. There is a surge of darkness coming over me. I can't explain it, but it is a thing I dread. I know the feeling too well, and when I feel it I know it is coming fast. Sometimes I feel nothing in advance and darkness comes all at once. Do I go to sleep then? And do I dream of things far removed from this room, this hospital bed, this keen awareness that I am clinging to life by the thinnest of threads?

I have no control over this, of course, but I hope I dream of something pleasant. I'd love to dream about heaven again. Or maybe dream I am a boy sitting on a wooded bluff looking out over the Ohio River. And maybe Uncle Dick will be there and we'll talk about Tom Sawyer and Huckleberry Finn and building rafts and floating down to Cairo.

If I sleep and dream, will I remember? If I sleep, will I wake? If my time is growing short, what comes next? I will trust in the words of Yeats: "I know that I shall meet my fate Somewhere among the clouds above . . . ." But what will be my fate? I wish I could hope for mercy, but my mind is filled with doubt. Mercy might lead me to a vast new world, over a distant peak. It is too distant, unless they give me wings, a summit I believe I'm destined never to reach.

36 / *Marilyn and Bucky*

JAN LEFT ROOM 12 shortly after the doctor's departure. She turned down the hall in one direction as Marilyn and Bucky approached from the other. Marilyn carried a large handbag, which dangled on a strap over her shoulder, and a pillow from the bed in her motel. Bucky carried a lidded container of coffee in each hand. They walked slowly, almost as if reluctant to reach the room where her husband and Bucky's best friend lay nearly as stiff and cold as a corpse in a shaft of sunlight that distorted the color of his white gauze bandages so that they might have been golden.

Bucky stopped at the foot of the bed. Marilyn stowed the pillow and her handbag on the wide chair against the wall and turned back to his side.

"It's hard," Bucky said. "I wish I could trade places with him. He's got you and the kids, and I have nobody who would miss me if I died tomorrow. I'm sorry, I didn't mean to make it sound like—"

"He's not going to make it, Bucky. The doctor has told me that from the beginning. Not as a certainty, but he wanted me to be prepared for it."

"Is Annie coming?"

"Yes, she said she'd be here this morning. I expect her to show up any minute."

"Did you ever get through to Craig?"

"No. All I can do is wait until he calls. But it doesn't matter, he probably wouldn't get here in time, anyway. They both know their father's wishes. No services, no burial. Cremation and scatter his ashes somewhere in the Shawnee National Forest."

"Are they okay with that?"

"I guess so. We've never talked about it."

"Are you?"

"It took me a while, but I'm good with it. I wouldn't want to take him back to Indiana or Chicago for burial and we haven't been anywhere else long enough to have any roots."

Bucky laughed. "I remember him saying once he wanted his body dumped in the Ohio River when he died. He said just let it float away and the fish would eat him up before he made it to the Mississippi. That was way back in Terre Haute. So long ago."

"He always had a fascination with the Ohio River. I guess it goes back to Uncle Dick's farm. He didn't have a lot going for him as a kid. I loved his mother but I never got a chance to know his grandmother. I met Uncle Dick a couple of times, and we went walking once or twice on Uncle Dick's farm. I'm not much of a nature girl, but it was very peaceful."

"Oh, yeah. Uncle Dick's farm and that damned little book of Tennyson poems his grandmother read from."

"I didn't know if you knew about the book."

"Heard about it a million times. And I don't mean to put it down like it sounded. I used to wish I had something like that to remember, know what I mean?"

"His grandmother's poetry made a lot of difference in his life. He was a kind and gentle man, like a poet, I guess. I wish I hadn't given him such a hard time over it. But he knew I didn't mean it."

Bucky turned and went to the window. He adjusted the shade to block part of the bright sun and stood looking to the west, where a cloud bank was forming. "It's going to rain before the day's done," he said. "Was that in the forecast?"

"Who pays attention to weather forecasts at times like this?"

"Marilyn, you know I love him like a brother."

"Yes. And he feels the same way about you. He has never stopped worrying about you."

Bucky turned to face her, then picked up the pillow and sat where it had been, on the chair, holding the pillow in his lap. He motioned for her and she came and sat beside him. He took her hand.

"There's something I have to ask you, Marilyn."

"Please, Bucky. Don't."

"But I want to know. And I think you already do. Did he have an affair with Nita?"

"I'm sorry, Bucky. He didn't know I knew, but I could tell his guilt was killing him—on top of all that happened in Vietnam. It didn't go anywhere, but yes, they did get involved. Nita told me. Just before she left, she came to see me and told me what went on. She was sorry, too, Bucky. She apologized to me and tried to take all the blame for it. I didn't buy that, of course. I told her it takes two to tango. But he didn't have to tell me. I know he was crushed at the thought he had broken up your marriage."

Bucky laughed, but with derision and not humor. "He didn't break up my marriage," he said. "He was just another notch on her garter. Nita has a weakness for men, and something happened to her after she lost our baby. She wanted men, like another man might mean another chance. She can't resist any guy who makes a move on her. But she covered her tracks pretty well. I think she really didn't want to humiliate me, and I know she actually had genuine affection for him, not like most of the others."

Marilyn pulled his hand up to her face and brushed it with her lips. "I'm sorry, Bucky. I had no idea."

"Like I said, she covered her tracks pretty well. She always looked up to you, Marilyn. She would not have wanted you to know, but she liked you too much not to feel guilty."

"I remember her last words to me. She said, 'Be well and have a good life.' And I knew she meant it."

"But you've known about them all this time? You've never shown any signs of it. How did you manage?"

Marilyn was drinking from one of the cups of coffee, and finished a long draught before she answered. "You'll lose all respect for me if I tell you."

"Never. I admire and respect you more than anyone else I know. You know that. I've always been a bit jealous of him for having you. I'm ashamed to say it, but after Nita left I had serious thoughts of trying to put a move on you. You know, to get revenge on him. But I couldn't do it that way, even though I've always found you very attractive. You know that, too."

"Yes, I know. Maybe we should have got together."

"But you wouldn't do that."

"Like hell! I'm not the angel you seem to think I am, Bucky. You asked how I got by. Well I got by by balling the shit out of a couple of guys who hung out at the gym. It was easy enough to rationalize away any problems of conscience. He did it to me first, right?"

Bucky's face displayed his surprise. But then he laughed. And this time it was genuine. "I'm afraid I don't know you as well as I thought. I would never have expected—"

"Simple, my good man. See, this guy here taught English literature, right? You know how he always comes up with a line from a favorite poet or some novelist to fit whatever occasion. Well, about the time I found out for sure about him and Nita I was reading one of the books he was teaching. Oscar Wilde. And the whole notion of the book was that we ought to throw away convention and give in to our temptations and enjoy them while we can. If you don't do it while you're young, you regret it when you get old but then it's too late."

"Damn! That's the kind of philosophy that could mess up society as we know it pretty quick, don't you think?"

"Maybe. But it worked for me when I needed it. The thing was, though, I couldn't talk to him about it for obvious reasons. If I could have, maybe he wouldn't have been so damned depressed over screwing up the life of his best friend. No pun intended. Remember that night Nita and I took him to the white room? He honestly was suicidal. And I think it was because we all had been drinking a bit and he'd been wanting to jump on Nita's bones all night, right in front of you. I do love this guy with all my heart, Bucky. I've tried to help him, or help him find help, but I just couldn't reach him."

Now it was Bucky who pulled her hand up to his face and kissed it softly. He sucked in his breath and held it for a moment, then released it in a sigh that was like a sign of resignation before he spoke.

"Marilyn, he was lost on a day in March of 1968 when he saw firsthand what hell really must be like. I doubt he ever has told you much about what happened that day. Right?"

"He never talked about the war."

"And you never made any effort to find out about that day?"

"The whole war thing—I tried. He just wouldn't talk about it. And I didn't want to push him too hard. There was always too much hurt. I just rationalized that when he was ready he would talk about it, and then over the years I hoped it had kind of gone away. But you say 'that day' like it all happened at once."

"It will never go away. And for him, it *was* pretty much all at once. That one day is why he probably never slept a single whole night without a nightmare, why he used to drink and take drugs, why little things would cause him to go into a rage sometimes, and why you guys ended up taking him to the white room that night while I was passed out on your bed because I have the nightmares, too."

"And you have just as much reason—"

"No! I saw too much combat, but I saw nothing like he saw that day. And took part in, at least to some extent. He may not have fired a single shot, but even if he didn't he thinks he did. And beyond that, I think it's likely that every man who saw it all go down feels guilty for doing nothing to try to stop it."

"Was it really that bad?"

"Marilyn, he was at My Lai."

She gasped. "My Lai! Bucky . . . My Lai . . . Oh, my god."

"You didn't know?"

"I never dreamed he had been through anything that bad. He never wanted to talk about the war, and I didn't want to push him. Oh, my god, Bucky. We all knew about the My Lai massacre, and why the protestors called them baby killers and all that. But I never had a clue he was there. Of course that was ancient history when we first met, but—"

"It will never be ancient history for him. One of the shrinks told me not even to try to forget what I'd seen because it was too deeply embedded in my brain. And what I saw was nothing next to what he saw at My Lai. They taught us to try to deal with it, not hope to forget it. They also warned us it might get worse as we got older, because that's when people kind of automatically tend to look back over the lives they've lived and all that."

Marilyn slipped down deeper into the chair. She leaned forward, and briefly buried her face in her hands.

"If I'd only known," she said. "Maybe he could have talked about it to me. All the dark moods. And it was getting worse. I thought it was about Nita, but now I know it wasn't. My Lai. Oh, my god, Bucky. He was at My Lai."

"We all wish we'd never heard of that place."

"I know it was bad, but I don't actually know what happened other than some lieutenant got court martialed for it. And I remember that when some of it came out it led to a lot more protests. And Kent State, I guess."

"Kent State was a couple of years after Me Lai, but things kept coming out that just fed the opposition to the war. Students on the college campuses got better organized and the bigger their numbers the easier it was for other kids to join in."

Marilyn folded her arms across her chest, as if in resignation. "It was ugly, wasn't it." She said this not as a question, but as a statement of fact, yet an invitation for him to tell her more.

"Yes. It was ugly. It's hard to imagine, really, how American soldiers could have done what they did that day in My Lai. But we can't put ourselves in their shoes. I won't judge them, Marilyn. I never have, and I told him that. I think he wanted to be judged, though. He wanted me to tell him how wrong it was, what they did. He wanted to be condemned. That's part of feeling guilty, I think. You want to hear what a terrible thing you've done so you can say how sorry you are."

"Can you tell me about it?"

Bucky moved close against her. He put an arm over her shoulders and pulled her close. She lay her head on his shoulder as he began to describe events that happened years earlier in a far-away place, in a war still being fought in the minds of too many men who were there when they happened.

"The men in Charlie Company, his unit, shot down more than five hundred Vietnamese civilians that day in My Lai," he said somberly. "Most of them were old people, women, and children. They shot them just like targets on the rifle range in training, except that these targets were living beings who in many cases stood facing them only yards away. They shot others in the back as they ran for their lives. And God forgive them, some men—soldiers in American uniforms—mutilated bodies of the fallen. It was cold-blooded slaughter."

"And nobody tried to stop it?"

"One of the helicopter pilots who flew them into the place to begin with landed his chopper between them and the villagers and had his gunner ready to cut down on the Americans if they didn't stop. But it was a little too late, I'd say. Everybody back in the day heard about the My Lai Massacre, but very few had a clue how bad it really was. The Army, the whole United States government, did everything they could to cover it up."

"And he was there. And took part, I guess."

"I don't know. I don't think he even knows for sure. But even if he didn't do any of the shooting himself, he watched his buddies do it. That's what he's been carrying all these years."

Marilyn shuddered, and pulled herself against Bucky even tighter. "It makes me sick even to think about it," she said. "I knew there were investigations and hearings and all that. He had to talk to some hearing officer once, but I never knew what it was about. I was too busy having a good time to be paying much attention to the war when all this actually happened, and there wasn't a lot of details about it in the news later. Or did I just miss it?"

"No, you didn't miss it because it wasn't there. It was the story nobody wanted to tell. The authorities managed to reduce everything to one trial and when it was over everybody just wanted to put it all behind them.

"He got hit a couple of days after it happened and hauled out to a field hospital and never returned to his unit, so he missed some of the aftermath. I think this probably saved him some of the hearings and all that, but it didn't erase the images from his mind."

"And this is where the 'baby killer' protests came from?"

"I guess. A lot of us who didn't do anything wrong paid a price for what his company did. They weren't the only ones, but My Lai set the standard, if that's the right word. And it's pretty easy for anyone who's never been in war to believe they wouldn't have acted that way."

Marilyn brushed the tears from her eyes with her fingertips, then took a tissue from a box on a shelf beside the window and wiped her eyes again and her nose. She was crying softly when she turned back to him. "Such a horrible thing to have to live with," she said. "And that's the guilt he's been carrying. God, Bucky! I wish I'd asked him about it more times, and maybe forced the issue when it might have helped."

"He wouldn't have told you."

For the next hour, neither of them talked. Medical people came and went. Bucky went down the hall to a rest room and when he came back Marilyn was slumped in the chair with her face buried in her hands, sobbing quietly. He told her they needed to go home and rest. "Home" meant back to their motel. Marilyn agreed, but asked him to come to her room when they got there because she didn't want to be alone.

Annie came right after they left, and spent an hour with her father. She sat close beside the bed and talked, mostly simple chit-chat because she knew he wouldn't hear. She talked about the children and told an old story about Aunt Sissy that he would have heard before. At one point she lay her head on his chest and cried.

A nurse Annie hadn't seen before came and asked if her mother was there, because Doctor Morrison wanted to talk with her. Annie told her no, her mother had come and gone for the day.

"She's worn out," Annie said. "I hope she gets some good rest tonight. This has been hard on her, as you probably understand."

"Absolutely. This is something a wife never should have to go through. I'm sorry. I should have said a daughter, too."

The nurse commenced some routine thing required of his medical care and Annie stepped aside so as not to be in her way.

"Look at this!" Annie exclaimed. "I've not seen one of these little guys for ages."

The nurse looked up. "What is it?"

"An inchworm. Here, let me put it on your sleeve. Daddy always told us if we found an inchworm it meant we were getting measured for new clothes."

The nurse stood still while Annie carefully picked up the little caterpillar from the windowsill and settled it on the blue-gray sleeve encasing her right arm. "I hope it works," she laughed. "My poor wardrobe is getting pretty skimpy."

"His grandmother told him it works," Annie declared, also laughing. "If it didn't, we can be confident somebody would have blown the whistle on it. You'll be the talk of the nurses' station in your new raiments."

The two women left the room together, comparing notes on family while walking down the hall.

37 / *An inchworm takes wing*

Two visitors who had not been there before, coming from opposite directions, reached the door of Room 12 at the same time. One was a tall and slender young man with long, unruly blonde hair and a full beard that almost reached his heart-line. The other was a woman, youthful-looking and pretty, with conspicuous weariness marking her face and an obvious hesitance as she neared the room. They studied each other warily for an instant, then spoke at once.

"Nita?"

"Yes, and you're Craig."

"It's been a long time. I wasn't sure it was you."

"Yes. It has been a long time. I didn't know if anyone would be here just now. Is there anyone else?"

He stood aside and motioned for her to enter ahead of him. The room was empty, except for the bed with its deathly still occupant and jungle of medical parapher-nalia on the back wall, overhead, and alongside the bed on both sides. Lighting had been reduced to a single glowing panel high on the back wall.

"I just got here," Craig told her. "I've been driving and flying for the last thirty-six hours. I know Mom's here and I think Annie is, but I haven't seen anyone."

"I'm glad I saw you first. Before anyone else, I mean. I don't know if I'm going to be welcomed, but I had to come. So what's with you? You look like you just walked off an adventure movie set or some such thing. What are you doing these days?"

"It's almost like that. Now don't laugh. I've been gold prospecting in Alaska."

Nita did laugh, but it was a sweet laugh of under-standing and acceptance. "You haven't changed," she said. "I'm glad, Craig. You've always walked your own walk. Your father has always been very proud of you for that."

"Now tell me about you. I thought you had dis-appeared from the face of the earth. Bucky—"

She put her finger to her lips.

"Don't mention any names," she pleaded. "I've not seen Bucky for years. Nor your mother. And of course not him."

"How did you know?"

"A former student of your father's works in Bucky's office. She and I have had an understanding all along and she knew I'd want to know. You knew I loved him, Craig. I still do."

She walked to the edge of the bed and put a hand on the rigid cast that encased the arm of the patient. Tears streamed down her cheeks.

Craig stepped close behind her, but stayed back a bit, away from the bed.

"Sweet is true love, though given in vain."

Nita took his hand. "You sound just like him," she said, squeezing his hand tightly. "He always has a bit of poem suitable to the occasion. Such a sweet and gentle man. You will be a credit to the human race if you turn out like him."

Craig slipped a small book from his pocket. "I could never be like him," he said. "But he taught me well. I always carry this. It's a little book of Tennyson poems that belonged to his grandmother."

He, too, stepped close against the side of the bed and put a hand on his father's arm. "You've been the best," he said. His voice was husky. "You taught me well. You told me, 'Knowledge comes, but wisdom lingers.' I didn't know it was Tennyson, but I should have guessed. The words could have been yours, though. I just happened onto the line in the little book of Tennyson poems I've carried with me all these years.

"I hope the throbbing war drums are quiet in your mind, Dad, and the battle flags furled in the Parliament of Man. Tennyson would want you to be at rest."

He bowed his head, in a motion of both grief and reverence.

Nita put a finger to her lips, then pressed the finger on the mummy-wrapped head of the man who lay before them. They stood a while longer, son and lover, then slipped away to find a secluded place where they could reminisce and plan to return at another hour.

It was late in the day. Rumbles of thunder could be heard and flashes of lightning were visible in the distance. Storms that had dropped heavy rains over wide swaths of the vast Illinois prairie earlier in the day had arrived at Memorial Hospital just before time for a change of nursing shift. Jan and a handful of others huddled in the hospital lobby for a few minutes, then rushed into the rain on their way to automobiles in a parking garage a hundred yards away.

Jan's emotional turmoil had become more intense as the day wore on. Phil would be home tomorrow, but for how long? He could be going off to war and she was not prepared for another long absence. This time, she was very much afraid it might be forever.

In the hospital cafeteria, a weary Doctor Arne Morrison took a seat at an out of the way corner table where a new entourage of eager students awaited his directions. He offered a welcoming smile. "We practice great medicine here," he told them. "We try to save lives, and often we do. But if you're serious about medicine, you have to begin by understanding there are no miracles."

Over their heads, in the tranquil solitude of a darkened Room 12 in the ICU on the sixth floor of Memorial Hospital's Wing C, a mortal existence was drawing to an end. Nature's demands that life be continuous already had been met; his blood flowed in the veins of Annie and Craig and generations yet to come.

And who could say? Might this not be the beginning of a new metamorphosis? Might not his spirit take wing, leaving the earthly realm behind and flying to new horizons with views of glories unimagined, immense new vistas where there is only poetry and music and kindness and forgiveness and gentleness and love? And if this comes to pass, will it not be a place beyond the grasp of mortals bent on war and destruction? And will his spirit not find ease at last?

The End

Other Books by Robert Hays

Fiction

A Shallow River of Mercy
Blood on the Roses
The Baby River Angel
The Life and Death of Lizzie Morris
Circles in the Water
Equinox and Other Stories
Early Stories from the Land (editor)

Non-Fiction

Patton's Oracle
Editorializing "the Indian Problem"
A Race at Bay
State Science in Illinois
G-2: Intelligence for Patton (with
Gen. Oscar Koch)
Country Editor

About the Author

Robert Hays is the author of five previous novels and has written, edited, or collaborated on a half-dozen works of non-fiction. His short stories have appeared in anthologies and he has published numerous academic journal and popular periodical articles. Selections from three of his novels have gained Pushcart Prize nominations. He is a U. S. Army veteran and, though retired from classroom teaching, holds professor emeritus rank on the faculty of the University of Illinois. He lives in the beautiful southern Illinois wooded hill country about which he writes.